DENISE CHÁVEZ

THE LAST OF THE MENU GIRLS

Denise Chávez is the author of *Loving Pedro Infante* and *Face of an Angel,* which won the American Book Award. She is the recipient of a Lila Acheson Wallace/Reader's Digest Fund Writer's Award and a founder of the Border Book Festival in Las Cruces, New Mexico, where she lives with her husband, Daniel Zolinsky.

THE LAST OF THE MENU GIRLS

THE LAST OF THE

MENU GIRLS

DENISE CHÁVEZ

VINTAGE CONTEMPORARIES

Vintage Books

A Division of Random House, Inc.

New York

First Vintage Contemporaries Edition, April 2004

Copyright © 1986, 2004 by Denise Chávez

All rights reserved under International and Pan-American
Copyright Conventions. Published in the United States by
Vintage Books, a division of Random House, Inc., New York,
and simultaneously in Canada by Random House
of Canada Limited, Toronto. Originally published
in slightly different form in the United States
by Arte Público Press, Houston, in 1986.

Vintage and colophon are registered trademarks
and Vintage Contemporaries is a trademark
of Random House, Inc.

Library of Congress Cataloging-in-Publication Data
Chávez, Denise.
The last of the menu girls / Denise Chávez.
p. cm.
ISBN 978-1-4000-3431-4
1. New Mexico—Social life and customs—Fiction. 2. Mexican American
families—Fiction. 3. Women—New Mexico—Fiction. 4. Girls—Fiction. I. Title.
PS3553.H346L3 2004
813'.54—dc22   2003069054

Book design by JoAnne Metsch

www.vintagebooks.com

Printed in the United States of America
10   9   8   7

Para mi madre,
Delfina Rede Faver Chávez,
quien baila en los cielos y
en los otros cuartos.

For my mother,
Delfina Rede Faver Chávez,
who dances in the sky and
in the other rooms.

CONTENTS

THE GREAT UNREST

There, at that place of recognition and acceptance, you will see the Marking-Off Tree at the edge of my world. I sit on the porch at twilight. The power is all around me. The great unrest twitters and swells like the erratic chords of small and large birds scaling their way home.

ROCÍO ESQUIBEL

It's been a long time since the publication of *The Last of the Menu Girls.*

I first wrote the collection as a graduate student at the University of New Mexico under the direction of Rudolfo Anaya, the novelist. I remember so much about the writing of the stories. I was living in Santa Fe and commuting to Albuquerque, the first Chicana writer to be the recipient of a Master's in Creative Writing fellowship offered by the English department.

"It'll only take one year," Rudy told me. It was too good to be true. "I'll take it," I said. And I did.

What I hadn't bargained for was the daily 120-mile round-trip commute, the scores of parking tickets, and a terrible case of walking pneumonia that left me in a dark tunnel for at least a year, no visible light at the end. I eventually moved to Albuquerque, coming home on weekends, but that didn't help. I was really sick. One night I was so bad off I asked Daniel, then my boyfriend, now my husband, to take me to the emergency room in Santa Fe to get an EKG. I knew my heart was in terrible condition. It had to be. I needed confirmation to let me know how really bad off I was. At St. Vincent's Hospital I was told my heart was fine, and I was sent home. With my newfound health, I asked Daniel to swing by the Sonic Drive-Inn for some celebratory onion rings. Being the kindhearted man he is, he complied with my request.

Many good things came about at that time. I met my husband. I got an M.A. in Creative Writing. I got to work with Tony Hillerman and Rudolfo Anaya, both mentors.

I remember where I wrote each story in this collection. "Evening in Paris" was written in bed with the flu, on a deadline for *Santa Fe Magazine,* in my house on Santa Rosa Street. "Compadre" was written in the cool shade of my mother's house one summer visit. The circumstances of each story is a story unto itself and likely will never be told, but I hold that time precious, as *The Last of the Menu Girls* was my first sustained piece of writing.

I remember I was always happily agitated with the stories, carrying them around as I did, a young writer who had never put together a collection, much less a book. "A book? You mean I have a book?" I asked Mr. Anaya.

All the stories were written out of the great love I have for my two home states, New Mexico and Texas. I wanted them to encompass the beauty, energy, and spirit of growing up between these two special worlds. My father, E. E. Chávez, was a New Mexican, born and bred, from a small town called Doña Ana. My mother, Delfina Rede Faver Chávez, came to all of us from an even smaller speck of a town called El Polvo (The Dust), Texas. Both of my parents' sensibilities and lives contributed much to the world of Rocío Esquibel and her struggle to find herself in the overwhelming blur of family.

Most of the stories were written for my Creative Writing workshop with Rudolfo Anaya and were suffused with the light and energy of New Mexico, but it was Texas that broadened and deepened the telling of Rocío's story. There is no place like Far West Texas, especially the Big Bend area, for giving light to my imagination.

So it is that these stories are bi-cultural, bi-lingual, and bi-magical renderings of my early memories and creations. They are not autobiographical in the full sense of the word, but touch upon a remembered accounting of what for me, as a young woman, were ideas and themes to be inspected, held close, revered or discarded.

Some critics call *The Last of the Menu Girls* a series of interconnected stories, others call it a novel. I think of the book in more theatrical terms and wish someone would come up with some sort of terminology to address this dramatic story structure that has its roots in theater.

Despite the challenge from Rudolfo Anaya to commit myself to a life of writing—a charge I didn't feel I was up to—I am happy with these honestly emotional vignettes which are scenes in a dramatic progression that ends with neighborhood handyman, Regino Suárez, breaking bread as a priest would, albeit with green chile.

I hadn't expected the first publication of *The Last of the Menu Girls* to go so smoothly. Little did I know that all the problems would arrive later on. I knew other writers who couldn't get their manuscripts read. I felt almost embarrassed to say how quickly a press became interested in my book. Those first few heady years after publication I was ignorant of the ramifications of the business of literature. In my naïveté I never imagined that the book could be tied up in litigation for nine years. It's a long story.

Only by the grace of God and my mother, a strong and determined woman who had faith in justice and in me, and who showed me by her example the power of just "sticking it out," was I able to endure the sadness of losing all rights to my book for those years. My mother was the epitome of someone who persevered, despite the odds, and it was through her belief in me that I was able to move through that challenging period. It tested my mettle, but it was also a time of growth; I always knew things would be resolved. They had to be.

In this revised edition, I have stayed true to what was for me the passion and magic of the early text, but have added clarification and depth where I felt it necessary. I've learned much about my writing style then and now. And the stories continue to delight and surprise me. And yes, some of them still make me cry.

Each story is complete unto itself but also connects to the larger whole that is Rocío's world. I took great care to link the stories in time and with attention to the seasons of my southwestern landscape. But these stories are rooted in more than their particular milieu, and, I hope, offer some truths for all to share.

I have reworked the order of the stories and feel much happier about their current placement. Somehow, in their first appearance, they got jumbled up independently of me. Now they seem to have found their true sequencing and moment in time.

It has been a joy to relive the vitality of Rocío's spirit as well as her willingness to ask the painful questions. She is a rebellious girl, but she doesn't have all the answers to life, and this may be what gives her a special, timeless vulnerability. Nieves Esquibel remains a rock and source of inspiration, and as I've aged I have come to appreciate the faithful Regio Suárez, anyone's best friend.

What is different about the two versions of this book? I would hope that the stories are cleaner, tighter. I feel more capable of making the direct statement. The articulation is easier and yet a bit more profound. To my great relief, I have released the punctuation I was once enamored of. I've left aside the dramatic dash and most of the exultant exclamation points. If anything, I have come to understand the use of the comma. I am still infatuated with ellipses. But periods are that. Periods. I'm older, bolder, less afraid.

If I were to write the stories now, I don't think they'd necessarily be better. I believe I know more about what the stories are about this time, although my early wisdom sometimes surprises me. The stories still strike me as trembling and alive, and for that I am grateful and relieved.

I hope you will enjoy Rocío's world and find in it the wonder of her name. She is the child of the morning dew, full of life, wondrous as a small child, and she is always filled with hope. She knows she is supported by the many sacred grounding energies: home, family, tradition, culture, landscape, and language. It's good to come back home to the basics.

DENISE CHÁVEZ
Las Cruces, New Mexico

THE   LAST   OF   THE   MENU   GIRLS

I was a child before there was a South. That was before the magic of the West, the beckoning of the North, or the West's betrayal. For me there was simply Up the street toward the spies' house, next to Old Man W's, or there was Down, past the Marking-Off Tree in the vacant lot that was the shortcut between worlds. Down was the passageway to family, the definition of small self as one of the whole, part of a past. Up was the direction of town, flowers.

My sister Mercy and I would scavenge the neighborhood for flowers that we would lay at Our Lady's feet during those long May Day processions of faith that we so loved. A white satin cloth would be spread on the floor. We would come up one by one and place our flowers on it, our breathless childish fervor heightened by the mystifying scent of flowers, the vision of flowers, the flowers of our offerings. It was this beatific sense of wonder that sent us roaming the neighborhood in search of new victims, as our garden had long been razed, emptied of all future hope.

On our block there were two flower spots: Old Man W's

and the Strongs'. Old Man W was a Greek who worked for the city for many years and who lived with his daughter, who was my older sister's friend. Mr. W always seemed eager to give us flowers; they were not as lovely or as abundant as the Strongs' flowers, yet the asking lay calmly with Old Man W.

The Strongs, a misnamed brother-and-sister team who lived together in the largest, most sumptuous house on the block, were secretly referred to by my sister and me as "the spies."

A chill of dread would overtake us as we'd approach their mansion. We would ring the doorbell, and usually the sister would answer our shaken inquiry with a lispy merciless "Yes?" She was a tall pale woman with a braided halo of wispy white hair who planted herself possessively in the door, her little girl legs in black lace shoes.

I always did the asking. In later years when the street grew smaller, less foreign, and the spies became, at the least, accepted, it was me who still asked questions, pleaded for flowers for Our Lady, me who heard the high, piping voices of ecstatic children singing, "Bring flowers of the fairest, bring flowers of the rarest, from garden and woodland and hillside and dale. . . ."

Their refrain floated past the high white walls of the church, across the Main Street irrigation ditch, and up our small street.

There was always Up the street and Down.

One always came Down.

Down consisted of all the houses past my midway vantage point, including the house across the street, occupied by a couple, the Carters, and their three small children, who later became my babysitting responsibilities, children whose names I have forgotten.

This is the house where one day a used sanitary napkin was ritually burned—a warning to those random and unconcerned depositors of filth, or so this is what one read in Mr. Carter's eyes as he raked the offensive item in a pile of leaves and dramatically set it on fire.

I peered from the trinity of windows cut in our wooden front door and wondered what all the commotion was about and why everyone seemed so stoically removed, embarrassed, or offended.

Later, babysitting for the Carters, I would mournfully peep from their cyclopean window and wonder why I was there and not across the street. In my mind I floated Down, past the Marking-Off Tree with its pitted green fruit. The tree was an Osage orange. Its fruit was useless, good for nothing but to throw or kick. Past the tree there were five or six houses, houses of strangers, "los desconocidos," as my grandmother used to say, "¿Y pues, quién los parió?"

From the Carters' window I would imagine looking back at our house as it was, the porch light shining, the lilies' pale patterns a diadem crowning the house at night.

The walk from the beginning to the end of the street took no longer than five or ten minutes, depending on the pace or the purpose of the walker. The walk was short if I was a messenger to my aunt's, or if I was meeting my father, who had recently divorced us and now called sporadically to allow us to attend to him. The pace may have been the slow, leisurely summer saunter with ice cream or the swirling dust-filled scamper of spring. Our house was situated in the middle of the block and faced a triangle of trees that became both backdrop and pivot points of this child's tale. The farthest tree, the Up Tree, was an Apricot Tree that was the property of all the neighborhood children.

The Apricot Tree stood in an empty lot near my cousin's house, cousin Florence who always got soap in her nose. She was always one of the most popular girls in school, and while I worshiped her, I was glad to have my nose and not hers. Our mothers would take turns driving us to our small Catholic school with a neighbor boy who my father nicknamed Priscilla because he was always with the girls.

Entering Florence's house on those days when it was her mother's turn to drive us, I would inevitably find her bent over the bathroom basin, sneezing. She would yell out, half snottily, half snortingly, "I have soap in my nose!"

Whether the Apricot Tree really belonged to Florence wasn't clear—the tree was the neighborhood's and as such was as familiar as our own faces, or the faces of our families. Her fruit, often abundant, sometimes meager, was public domain. The tree's limbs draped luxuriously across an irrigation ditch whose calm, muddy water flowed all the way from the Río Grande to our small street where it was diverted into channelways that led into the neighborhood's backyards. The fertile water deposited the future seeds of asparagus, weeds, and wildflowers, then settled into tufted layers crossed by sticks and stones—hieroglyphic reminders of murky beginnings.

Along with the tree, we children drew grateful power from the ditch's penetrating wetness. The tree was resplendent with offerings—there were apricots and more—there were the sturdy compartments, the chambers and tunnelways of dreams, the stages of our dramas. "I'm drowning!

I'm drowning!" we called out as we hung from the limbs, and were saved at the last moment by a friendly hand. "This is the ship and I am the captain!" we exulted after having transcended our mock deaths.

Much time was spent at the tree, alone or with others. All of us, Priscilla, Soap-in-Her-Nose, the two dark boys Up the street, my little sister, and I, all of us loved the tree. We would often find ourselves slipping off from one of those choreless, shoreless days, and with a high, surprised "Oh!" we would greet each other's aloneness, there at the tree that embraced us all.

Returning home, we may have wandered alongside the ditch, behind the Westers' house, and near the other vacant lot that housed the second point of the triangle, the Marking-Off Tree, the likes of which may have stood at the edge of the Garden of Eden. It was dried-up, sad. All the years of my growing up it struggled to create a life of its own. The tree passed fruit every few years or so—as old men and women struggle to empty their ravaged bowels. The gray-green balls that it brought forth we used as one uses an empty can, to kick and thrash. The tree was a reference point, offering no shade, but always inviting meditation. It delineated the Up world from the Down. It marked off the nearest home, without being home; it was a landmark, and as such, occupied our thoughts, not in the way the Apricot Tree did, but in a subtler, more profound way. Seeing the tree was like seeing the viejito downtown for so long, tape on his neck, the voice box gargling a sound, his face full of bruises, his unsteady hand holding his bottle, and thinking "How much longer?"

There, at that place of recognition and acceptance, you

will see the Marking-Off Tree at the edge of my world. I sit on the front porch at twilight. The power is all around me. The great unrest twitters and swells like the erratic chords of small and large birds scaling their way home.

To the left is the Willow Tree. How to introduce her?

How can I show you a love that is without words?

All I ever knew or understood as a child was the large looming presence of family. My world was bound by family. And to me, the Willow Tree was my closest kin.

To introduce the Willow Tree I have to introduce my sister who lived in France and her husband who died when he was only thirty. They would both be standing in front of the tree, holding hands. I would show you a glimpse of their eternal charm, their look and stance, the intrinsic quality of their bloom.

You would see inside a family album a black-and-white photograph of a man with a wide, ruddy face, in shirtsleeves, holding a plump, squinting child in front of a small tree, a tree too frail to endure, surely.

On the next page an older girl passes a hand through windblown hair and looks at you. You can feel her gentle beauty, love her form. Next to her a young girl stands, her small eyes turned toward her godfather, who stares at the photographer, now shaded by a growing-stronger tree. Or you would be at a birthday party, one of the guests, rimmed in zinnias, cousins surrounding—Soap-in-Her-Nose, the two dark boys (younger than in story time), and the others—miniaturized versions of their future selves. Two sisters with their arms around each other's child—delicate necks stand out—as the warps and twinings of the willow background confuse the boys with their whips and the girls with their fans.

In this last photograph, one sees two new faces, one shy boy huddled among the girls, the other sun-blinded, lost in leaves.

The Althertons—Rob, Sandy, Ricky, and Randy—lived next to us. The history of the house next door was wrought with struggle. Before the Althertons moved in, the Cardozas had lived there, with their smiling young boys, senseless boys, demon boys. It was Emmanuel (Mannie) who punched the hole in our plastic swimming pool and Jr. who made us cry. Toward the end of the Cardoza boys' reign, Mrs. C, a small, breathless bug-eyed woman, gave birth to a girl. Mr. C's tile business failed, and the family moved to Chiva Town, vacating the house for the Althertons, an alternately histrionically dry and loquacious couple with two boys. Ricky, the oldest, was a tall, tense boy who stalked the Altherton spaces with the natural grace of a wild animal, ready to spring, ears full of sound, eyes taut with anticipation. Young Randy was a plump boy-child with deep, watery eyes that clung to Mrs. Altherton's lumpish self, while lean and lanky Papa A ranged the spacious lawn year-round in swimming trunks, searching for crabgrass, weeds, any vestiges of irregularity. Lifting a handful of repugnant weed, he'd wave it in the direction of Sandy, his wife, a pigeon of a woman, who cooed, "You don't say. . . ."

Jack Spratt could eat no fat, his wife could eat no lean, and between them both, you see, they licked the platter clean. . . .

The Altherton yard was very large, centered by a metal pole to which was attached the neighborhood's first tetherball. From the porch, where my sister and I sat dressing dolls, we could hear the punch and whirr of balls, the crying and calling out. Ricky would always win, sending Randy racing inside to Mrs. A's side, at which time, having dispatched his odious brother, Ricky would beat and thrash the golden ball around in some sort of crazed and victorious adolescent dance. Randy and Mrs. A would emerge from the house, and they would confer with Ricky for a time. Voices were never raised. The two plump ones would then go off, hand in hand, leaving the lean to himself. Ricky would usually stomp away down the neighborhood, flicking off a guiltless willow limb, deleafing it in front of my watchful eyes, leaving behind his confused steps a trail of green, unblinking eyes, the leaves of our tree.

Every once in a while Randy would walk over to us as we sat dressing dolls or patting mud pies, and hesitantly, with that babyish smile of his, ask us to come and play ball. We two sisters would cross the barriers of Altherton and joyfully bang the tetherball around with Randy. He played low, was predictable, unlike Ricky, who threw the ball vehemently high, confounding everyone.

Ricky's games were over quickly, his blows firm, surprising, relentless. Ricky never played with my sister and me. He was godlike and removed, like our older sister, already sealed in some inexplicable anguish of which we children had no understanding. It was Randy who brought us in, called out to us, permitted us to play. And when he was not there to beckon us, it was his lingering generosity and gentleness that drew us into the mysterious Altherton yard, allowing us to risk fear, either of Mr. Altherton and his perennial tan, or Ricky with his senseless animal temper. Often we would find the yard free and would enjoy the tetherball without interruption; other times we would see Ricky stalk by, or hear the rustling approach of clippers, signifying Mr. Altherton's return. If we would sense the vaguest shadow of either specter, we would run, wildly, madly, safely home, to the world of our Willow, where we would huddle and hide in the shelter of its green labyrinthine rooms, abstracting ourselves from the world of Ricky's torment or Mr. Altherton's anxious wanderings.

I have spoken least of all of the Willow Tree, but in speaking of someone dead or gone, what words can reach far enough into the past to secure a vision of someone's smiling face or curious look? Who can tame the restless past and show, as I have tried to show, black-and-white photographs of small children in front of a tree?

The changes in the Willow were imperceptible at first. Old Man W, the Greek, through an oversight in pronunciation, had always been Mr. V. The spies became individualized when Mr. Strong later became my substitute history teacher and caused a young student to faint. She was afraid of blood, and had looked up into the professor's nose, where she saw unmistakable flecks of red. The two dark boys grew up, became wealthy, and Soap-in-Her-Nose moved away. The irrigation ditch was eventually closed. Only the Willow remained—consoling, substantial. The days became shorter and divided the brothers while the sisters grew closer.

Ricky, now a rampaging adolescent, continued his thoughtless forays, which included absently ripping off willow limbs and discarding them on our sidewalk.

"He's six years older than Randy," said my mother, that dark mother who hid in trees. "He just never got over Randy's birth; he hates his brother. You love your sister don't you, Rocío?"

"Yes, Mother," I would say.

It was not long after Ricky's fourteenth birthday that the Willow began to ail, even as I watched it. I knew it was hurting. The tree began to look bare. The limbs were lifeless, in anguish, and there was no discernible reason. The solid, green walls of our child's play collapsed, the passageways became cavernous hallways, the rivers of grass dried, and there was no shade. The tree was dying. My mother became concerned. I don't know what my little sister thought; she was a year younger than me. She probably thought as I did, for at that time she held me close as model and heroine, and enveloped me with her love, something Randy was never able to do for his older brother, that bewildered boy.

It wasn't until years later (although the knowledge was there) that my mother told me that one day she went outside to see Ricky standing on a ladder under our Willow. He was ripping whole branches off the tree and furiously throwing them to one side.

Mother said, "What are you doing, Ricky?"

He replied, "I'm killing the tree."

"You're killing it?" she responded calmly.

It is here that the interpretation breaks down, where the photographs fade into gray wash, and I momentarily forget what Ricky's reply was that day so many years ago, as the limbs of our Willow fell about him, cascading tears, willow reminders past the face of my mother, who stood solemnly by without horror.

Later, when there was no recourse but to cut down the tree, Regino Suárez, the neighborhood handyman, and his son were called in.

Regino and his son had difficulty with the tree; she refused to leave the earth. When her roots were ripped up, there lay a cavity of dirt, an enormous aching hole like a tooth gone, the sides impressed with myriad twistings and turnings. The trunk was moved to the side of the house, where it remained until several years ago, when it was cut up for firewood, and even then, part of the stump was left.

Throughout the rest of grade school, high school, and college—until I went away, returned, went away—the Willow stump remained underneath the window of my old room.

Often I would look out and see it there, or on thoughtful walks, I would go outside near the Althertons' old house, now sealed by a tall concrete wall, and I would feel the aging hardness of the Willow's flesh.

A painful, furrowed space was left in the front yard, where once the Willow had stood. It filled our eyes, my sister's, Mother's. The wall of trees, backdrop to the traveling me, that triangle of trees—the Apricot Tree, the Marking-Off Tree, the Willow Tree—was no longer.

One day Ricky disappeared, and we were told that he'd been sent to a home for disturbed boys.

As children we felt dull, leaden aches that were voiceless and incommunicable cries. The place they sprang from seemed so desolate and uninhabited and did not touch on anything tangible or transferable. Children carry pain in that particular place, that wordless, gray corridor, and are unable to find the syllables with which to vent their sorrow. They are unable to see, yet able, willing and yet unwilling . . . to comprehend. A child's sorrow is a place that cannot be visited by others. Always the going back is solitary, and the little sisters, however much they loved you, were never really near, and the mothers, well, they stand, as I said, solemnly, without horror, removed from children by their understanding.

I am left with recollections of pain, of loss, with holes to be filled. Time, like trees, withstands the winters, bursts forth new leaves from the dried old sorrow—who knows when and why—and shelters us with the shade of later compassions, loves, although at the time the heart is seared so badly that the hope of all future flowerings is gone.

Much later, after the death of the Willow, I was walking to school when a young boy came up to me and punched me in the stomach. I doubled over, crawled back to Sister Elaine's room, unable to tell her of my recent attack, unprovoked, thoughtless, insane. What could I say to her? To my mother and father? What can I say to you? All has been told. The shreds of magic living, like the silken green ropes of the Willow's branches, dissolved about me, and I was beyond myself, a child no longer. I was filled with immense sadness, the burning of snow in a desert land of consistent warmth.

I walked outside today, and the same experience repeated itself—oh, not the same form, but yes, the attack. I was the same child, you see, mouthing pacifications, incantations. . . .

"Bring flowers of the fairest, bring flowers of the rarest . . .
It's okay . . .
From garden and woodland and hillside and dale . . .
Our pure hearts are swelling . . .
It's alright . . .
Our glad voices telling . . .

Please . . .

The praise of the loveliest rose of the dale. . . ."

Jack Spratt could eat no fat, his wife could eat no lean, and between them both, you see, they licked the platter clean. . . .

My mother planted a willow several years ago, so that if you sit on the porch and face left, you will see it thriving. It's not in the same spot as its predecessor, too far right, but of course, the leveling was never done, and how was Regino to know? The Apricot Tree died, the Marking-Off Tree is fruitless now, relieved from its round of senseless birthings. This Willow Tree is new. It stands in the center of the block . . . between . . .

THE CLOSET

I

When I close my eyes I can see Christ's eyes in the darkness. It's an early-summer afternoon, and I should be sleeping. Instead, I'm standing in the silence of my mother's closet holding a luminescent sliding picture of the Shroud of Turin. One image reveals Christ as he might look fleshed out; the other shows shadows of skin pressed against white cloth. A slant of light filters through the closed door.

"It's my turn! Let me in! I want to see!"

Mercy whispers impatiently from behind the door. In the half-tone darkness my eyes travel from the wedding photograph at the back of the closet to the reality of my mother's other life. Shoes crowd the floor, teacher's shoes, long comfortable plastic loafers, sandals, and open-toed pumps in blue and black, the sides stretched to ease the bunions' pressure. They are the shoes of a woman with big feet, tired legs, bitter hopes. They are the shoes of someone who has stood all her life in line waiting for better things to come.

"Mother! Mother!" I yelled one day across a downtown shoe store. "Is size ten too small?"

She answered me with an impatient look, as if she'd pinched me and no one had seen what she'd done, a look reserved for nasty children who'd had the audacity to perform obscenities in public. She scowled across the crowded store, "No! And don't yell, your voice carries!"

Mother was married to a man who bathed twice a day. Juan Luz Contreras was very clean. He was the town's best catch, a descendant of the Contreras family of West Texas. Head 'em up. Round 'em up. Ride 'em out. Dead. Juan Luz was poisoned by an unscrupulous druggist—oh, unwittingly. He was forced to drink acid. Someone poured it down his throat, but why? He had a wife and a child only three days old. His wife was my mother.

For many years I wondered who the man in the wedding photo was at the back of my mother's closet. He wasn't my father. My father still lived with us at that time, but he wasn't home much. Who was the man in the photograph if he wasn't my father? Later I found out he was Juan Luz, my mother's first husband, my older sister Ronelia's father.

When my father finally left our home, it was Juan Luz's face in the crowded closet who comforted me. From all accounts he was a perfect man.

Standing in the closet, I can smell the pervasive loneliness of my mother, in her flowered bathrobes and suits of gradually widening girth. It is the soft, pungent woman smell of a fading mother of three girls, one of them the daughter of the unfortunate Juan Luz.

The portrait of my mother and Juan Luz is hidden behind piles of clothes that are crowded into the largest closet in the house. All those memories are now suffocated in cloth. So whoever comes, whatever man comes, and only *one* could, he would not feel alarm. But would my father come, being gone so long?

I remember the nights my father was home, sitting in his favorite red chair, reading the evening newspaper and later telling stories to my sister Mercy and me.

"A is for Aardvark and In the Name of the Father and the Son and Little Lulu and Iggy went to the store. . . . And what did you learn at school today, baby?"

Sometimes, alone on the armchair or on his lap, I recounted tales of Dick and Jane and little blond-haired Sally.

"Please, Daddy, tell me the story of the two giant brothers, Hilo and Milo."

When I open my eyes, I return to the darkness of the closet. With small feet, I stand on my mother's shoes. I could never fill them even if I tried.

If I didn't hold the body of Christ in my hands and if there wasn't anything to glow in the dark and then to disappear, I could see faces in the closet and hear people talking and feel alone. I'm afraid in the middle of the day. Me, supposed to be taking a nap in August and it being the hottest month to be born in and with a crying baby sister outside the door yell-whispering, "Come on, it's my turn!"

And there I'd be, holding on to the brass-colored knob with one hand, and Mercy yanking with both, and the Shroud of Turin in my left hand getting crumpled and there I'd be, whispering, "Shut up, shut up! She'll hear you and so I'm looking, okay? It's *my* turn! Okay?"

The boxes are open and soon scarves and hats will be all over the floor and I'll have to get a chair and put them up on the top shelf and while I'm up there I'll look at the cloth flowers and then the feathers and I might want to play dress-up with the hats.

"We'll listen to the records on the top shelf, Mercy. 'The Naughty Lady of Shady Lane' and 'Fascination.' We'll dance like we like to dance. We'll be floating ballerinas meeting each other midway under the tropical-bird-like fixture. You can practice your diving while I count the flowers, arranging them in rows and humming, 'Let me go, let me go, let me go, lover,' while you rest from your long swim."

"It's my turn, Rocío, you get to look at the Christ eyes all the time!"

"There's no eyes, only sockets!"

"If I squint Chinesey, I can see eyes."

"Yeah?"

"So let me have the thing, it's my turn. You always look too long."

"You might get scared, baby."

"Me, no—you promised."

"Baby, baby, baby! There's no eyes, only sockets!"

"Open that door, you promised!"

"Go ahead, baby, come inside, here's the light!"

I turn the light on Christ and Juan Luz and my mother and all my dark secret young girl thoughts and face my little Sally sister with her baby-limp hair.

"Go ahead Mercy baby! Take the stupid thing. But let me look one more time."

I yank on the old pink-and-chartreuse belt that has become my mother's light cord, and go back inside the closet for one last look. I stumble across the gift box, full of vinyl wallets and heart-shaped handkerchiefs and a plastic container of car- and animal-shaped soap. The gift box is regularly replenished by my mother's elementary school students' Christmas and birthday gifts: "Merry Christmas, love Sammy." "To Teacher from Mary." "You are nice, Mrs. Esquibel, I'll never forget you. Bennie Roybal. 1956."

I turn off all the lights and close the door as tight as I can. I look at the glow-in-the-dark Jesus card and slide it back and forth. The skeleton color of yellow-white bone is electrified, and I can feel and see the Christ eyes in the almost total darkness.

"So here it is, baby! Leave me alone. I'm going to lie down on the bed and rest. Don't bother me and remember, this is the invisible line, your side, and mine. Don't cross over like you do, with those rubbery hairy spidery legs of yours. Here, see the pillow? Gosh, if we had a yardstick it would be good, but anyway, this pillow divides me from you, my side from yours, okay, baby? I want the side by the wall and the pictures. So that when I'm drifting off to sleep, I can look at Ronelia in her wedding dress when she was seventeen years old and just married. She wore Mother's dress and Mother's veil, well, maybe not the veil, but the little plastic pillbox crown with wax flower buds. Maybe you and I will someday wear that dress, Mercy, okay? Okay? What do you think?"

"Oh, leave me alone!" she says.

As I lie in bed, Mamá Consuelo and her husband stare at

me from across the room. Their faces are superimposed on wood. It's more than a photograph. It's a carved picture of two people, one of them a stranger. I don't ever know what to call my grandfather. I never called him and he never called me. So he doesn't have a name. But he's my grandfather. He was strong. He was good. He worked hard during the depression. He was better off than most. And he died in his sleep from a blood clot or brain hemorrhage. All I know is that he had a headache, leaped over my sleeping grandmother in the middle of the night to take an aspirin, and then went back to sleep and never woke up. About Mamá Consuelo I know more.

"Oh, Mercy, sleeping in the afternoons makes me tired. Without something to do or think about, I'll really fall asleep. I might as well get the crown of thorns down from the crucifix and try them on."

"Are you sure, Rocío? Shouldn't you leave them alone?"

Over Mother's bed there's a crucifix, and on the crucifix there's a crown of thorns. Real thorns, like the ones Christ was crowned with, only these are very small and they cover just the center of my head, the baby spot. It doesn't matter they're baby-sized, because when I push them down I feel what Christ felt. Oh, they hurt, but not too much. I never pushed them down all the way. But I can imagine what they feel like. They have long waxy spikes with sharp tips. I can imagine the rest. I've been stabbed by pencils in both my palms. The one on my right looks like one of the stigmata.

Naps. I hate naps because there's so much to do and think and feel, especially in August. If I have to sleep, I like it to be quick and over with before I know it, or long and happy with a visit to the Gray Room.

The Gray Room is a place I visit when I'm alone. The Gray Room was before my littleness, before my fear of cloth shadows from clothing on chairs, or the animals the shadows made.

It began when I was a very young girl. I was never afraid. Every day I visited a world that the others knew nothing about. Not Ronelia, not my mother, not my father, not even Mercy.

No one knew I lived in the Gray Room or that I flew through air and time. I entered the Gray Room late at night, when the house was quiet and I was alone. I'd crawl through the hall closet and into the concrete passageway that was our house's foundation. Down I would go, into the unfinished space below the house, inching my way into the awesome darkness, alone, unhampered, guided more or less by a voice that pulled me and drew me, further, further, into the concrete maze. The space became larger, a room of immense proportions, a high room, an altar room, a sanctuary where I was the only devout communicant. Higher, higher I climbed, past the attic, to the labyrinth that was the Gray Room. This world was my refuge—this world unknown to anyone!

Each step was a step forward into that other world, the world of concrete corridors, the endless labyrinths, a soundless foray into a maze of faceless forms, living spirits. They led into the heart and spirit of the house. When the spirit was sick, the nocturnal journey was long, the gasping for air at the bottom of an endless summer pool. When the spirit was pure, a long rope flew down and I was beamed up on an umbilical cord of light. I flew beyond the Gray Room into the Blue Room and farther up, into the vast No Room of the living sky. Up beyond worlds, I flew into a universe of change, to the No Place of dreamers who do not dream.

One day I began to live two separate lives. One magical, the other fearful. I woke up screaming, "The animals! The animals!" From deep within myself I heard the foggy mist of concerned voices. No one understood. Mother was afraid for me. And I was afraid as well.

"But you wouldn't understand, Mercy! You'd say, 'The closet! There's nothing under our house, no rooms, no space for you to crawl through. There's no house above or underneath our house. There's no huge room without a ceiling! But Mercy, I've *been* there. I've spoken to the Keeper of the Room. He's an animal and brown. He wanted to make the room smaller, but I said no. I told him, 'There's no space for you, go away!' "

Now the room is white and blue and mine, alone.

All this came to me in dreams. I felt presences and heard voices and the sound of breathing and music far away, then near. There was smoke in my room; I couldn't breathe. The animals crowded into corners. I woke up in the middle of the night, trying to run away. Mother turned on the hall light to check in on me and give me a baby aspirin. I drifted off again.

"Walking in your sleep" Mother called it.

"Mercy, would you believe me if I told you that I was born in a closet?"

"Rocío, you're crazy!"

Mother was forty years old. She'd been a widow nine years. A table was brought into the room, but the legs were removed because the doorway was too small. When I was born, Mother and I came crashing down. I shot into a closet full of shoes, old clothes. It was 4:48 A.M. on a hot August day. Ronelia hung outside the door. She was nine years old, too young to see such things.

Later, I imagined the wood, the splinters, the darkness, and the shoes. And yet, on playing back the tape, Mercy, I always play back love. Much love.

I heard voices that said: "We are the formless spirits who take form, briefly, in rooms, and then wander on. We are the grandmothers, aunts, sisters. We are the grandfathers, uncles, brothers. We are the women and men who love you."

"Oh my God, Mercy, do you understand these things?"

No amount of tears will ever wash the pain or translate the joy. Over and over, it's the same, then as now. Birth and Death. There's me, in the Gray Room, or in the closet with the shoes.

"Mercy, remember the closets, remember them?"

II

The bathroom closet was full of ointments, medicines, potions to make us softer, more beautiful, less afraid. It held vials to relieve us, deceive us. It was the mysterious healing place, the place of bandages, Mercurochrome, and cotton balls.

The center section contained the "good" towels, only

used for company. They sat in their special pile, waiting for the occasional party, the welcome stranger, the annual holiday. They waited for that overnight guest or beloved family member, for nights of rearranged beds, noise, and laughter.

Below this were the special blankets and the sheets, all folded tidily. On the higher shelf were filmy containers of generic aspirin that were consumed candylike by Mother, for headaches, backaches, heartaches.

In the corner was an unused snakebite kit, with its rubber hand pump and arm tie. Mercy and I fantasized this ordeal and practiced what to do if that time should come. The *one* time presented itself. We were in Texas, on the way to Big Bend National Park. The two of us had gotten out of the crowded car to stretch. We had walked a ways into the scrub brush when we heard the sound of a rattler. And there we were, three hundred miles from home!

I looked at and then talked to that snake. And then I ran, wildly, madly, all the way back to the car. What did you do, Mercy? I knew we could have died. One of us at least. It would have been me, because I was closest to the snake and saw him first. We drove on, the boy cousins up front, the girl cousins in back. I know it would have been me.

The snakebite kit was still in the closet, next to a greasy baby oil bottle. We never had suntan lotion until we were older, as we never had artichokes to eat, or eggplant or okra. We had summer dreams of swimming all day long, until our eyes were red, our toes and fingers pruney, and our crotches white and soft and surrounded by browned skin.

Earlier we had taken a shortcut near the Marking-Off

Tree. The shortcut led to a world of water games: splish-splash, tag, dibble-dabble. You were the swimmer, Mercy, and I the observer.

In my dreams I was always surfacing, having swum from an almost fatal underwater voyage. Later I stood in the darkened shade of the small blue-and-white bathroom, peeling off my bathing suit like a layer of skin. My body was ice-cold and excited, slightly damp.

I changed into summer clothes: shorts, a cotton top, and thongs. My hair was wet, in curled strips, my lips were full, my cheeks tanned, my eyes wild and smaller than normal size. My wet, slithering body found comfort in cloth. I felt a great and immense hunger, as swimmers do, especially children. I took a towel from the closet, the white ones bordered in black that we were allowed to use, and saw from the corner of my eye a vodka "miniature" placed there by my father, who was always hiding them. He no longer lived with us, but I found his bottles everywhere, in his old chest of drawers, under my mother's bed. The bathroom smelled of my cool flesh, of Vicks and liquor, of old prescriptions for ever-present maladies.

In the closet were remedies for my mother's womanly ailments: hardened waxy suppositories, blood-pressure tablets, weight pills, sulfa drugs, cough medicines, and aspirins of all sizes and shapes. There were medications for the head, the rectum, the stomach, the bladder, the eyes, the heart. The old shaving lotion was a reminder that we lived in a house of women.

An enema bag, salmon-colored and slightly cracked, the nozzle head black and foreboding, was poised and ready to be used. The last time Mother gave me an enema I was twelve, not yet a woman, but old enough to be embarrassed. I was sick, too tired to fight. Vicks and the smell of my discomfort intermingled.

At sixteen, I sucked in the hot pleasant forbidden cigarette smoke and blew it out of the wire screens, hoping it would disappear. The butts were dispatched in the usual two ways—flushed away or wrapped in Kleenex. I lit matches hoping the sulfur smell would mask my sins. But Mother knew. Mother took her aspirin so she wouldn't have to worry about me while I smoked nude on the toilet, blowing out smoke through the mesh screen.

The bathroom closet held my sexual adolescent dreams. It was full of necessities and bodily functions. Everyone hid there.

It was there I smoked my first cigarette, read letters from a lost lover, and reverently held my mother's old used diaphragm.

III

I smelled Johnny. Johnny again. Johnny accidentally left his blue sweatshirt jacket in the living room over Christmas vacation for three long weeks. I hung it in my closet, next to my clothes. When I closed the door I smelled Johnny, the undefinable sweetness of his young maleness.

"Oh God, Rocío, you are so gross! You are the grossest girl I know!"

"Oh settle down, just settle down, Mercy, would you?"

The smells of my closet are lusty and broad: the smells of body odors and special juices and the memory of slithering afterbirths. This is where I slid—into the closet full of shoes.

The closet smelled of summer and long nights and swollen red lips and burned bobby socks. I washed them every night and dried them on the floor furnace in the hallway outside my room.

They were my one and only pair of bobby socks. I bought them across the street from my school, at the Mott's Five and Dime. One day I accidentally burned them beyond hope. Mortified and angry with myself, I took them up to the attic to hide them.

My passions and fantasies were lost in time that way—stuffed into dark corners as I attempted to forget what bothered me. And yet, the truth I speak is not an awkward truth. I treasured the smells and touches and the darkness of that time. That time of the bathroom closet. It was a receptacle for a me I always wanted to be, knew I could become: a woman, not at all like my mother.

IV

The TV room closet was Ronelia's. Her old strapless prom dresses were there, her evening gowns of tulle, with their spaghetti straps. The closet was immense and covered the entire side of the wall that faces away from the door. It was built by Regino Suárez, the neighborhood handyman. The wooden doors never opened without a struggle and got stuck midway, so that you had to push one way and then the other to get inside. In this closet were stored long dresses, costumes, and party shawls with Mother's notations: "Summer Long." "Ronelia's Party." "Wedding Dress, Nieves's." Alongside were her initials and the date. "Ronelia FHA Queen. 1955. Yellow Tulle, N.E."

The long cardboard boxes were crammed onto the top shelf, and below them in pink and blue plastic clothing bags were the furs, the beaver Tío Frutoso trapped himself, the suede with the soft fur neck piece, the beige imitation fur coat Mercy wore as a little girl, and Mamá Consuelo's prized muff. The closet smelled of old petticoats and musty fur. It stored two wedding dresses, a new one and an old one. The new one Mother picked up at a sale for five dollars. The old one she wore when she married Juan Luz. Ronelia and Mercy later wore that dress, but it was usually carefully sealed in plastic at the very bottom of the top shelf. Anything to do with Juan Luz—photographs, articles of clothing, papers— were sacred and off-limits. To me, they were the Ark of the Covenant—full of mysterious untouchability. I was ignorant of the past and the relationship of my mother to this man, long since dead.

Children assign mystery to small objects and create whole worlds from pieces of cloth. This closet, then, was a glistening world of dances and proms and handsome dates. It was Ronelia's wedding at the age when most of us are still children. The closet meant life to me, the world of the dance. It contained my Zandunga costume, the dress I wore when I danced with Mercy as my "male" partner for bazaars and fiestas.

"Ay, Zandunga, Zandunga, mamá, por dios. . . . Ay Zandunga . . . Zandunga . . ."

The closet was Nieves at her best, her finest, and Mercy

in imitation beige fur with a silk lining. The closet held two brides, one eternally wedded, the other, husbandless.

V

The living room closet held the house umbrella in rainbow colors. For many years there was but this one umbrella, large, sturdy, friendly. It came out on late-summer afternoons when we played outside in the rain. It welcomed and protected guests who came to visit during early-fall rainstorms. It shielded us in the middle of the summer heat when the fierce wildness of the unleashed summer tensions rose and fell. The umbrella was the symbol and hope of rain. To desert souls rain is the blessed sex of God. It cleanses and refreshes. It is the best mother, the finest lover.

The rainbow umbrella emerged, unhooked from its long nail and opened outside. It dried on the porch, each time a little grayer. One day it was replaced in black, by one of its funereal sisters.

The living room closet was the "guest" closet. It held all coats except Johnny's, which had found a dearer resting place. Overflow "good" clothes, from the fancy dress and coat closet, were placed in here as well. Christmas and birthday gifts were hidden in the gift box. Paper bags full of rummage and used clothing were stored inside, too, on their way south. The closet was a clearinghouse—the "outgoing" closet, the last stop before dispersal—to needy families in México, young marrieds who had little and senior citizens who used the hand-sewn rugs Nieves made especially for them.

The closet was full of seasonal smells: summer rain, damp

dark winter coats, the faint odor of Avon perfume like dried autumn flowers, the spring smell of soap and freshness. It smelled, too, of luggage and time, of faded newspapers, of my grandfather's handmade cane and the slippery chalk Mother used to mark the hems on our ever-shortening skirts.

Behind the door were dated check stubs and much-used prayer books. The door had its own smell of wood and fingerprints. The ceiling had a trapdoor that for me was another path to the Gray Room. The closet was but another valve leading to the many chambers of the house's heart, where I lived my other life, with its own separate heartbeat.

VI

My mother Nieves's closet was her life, her artery of hope. Its corners were hers, unviolated. In the back, on the right side, behind her clothes, was her wedding photograph. She and Juan Luz, both slim, with bright, serious faces, stared out at the photographer. Behind them was a stairway, a mirror on each side, which seemed to lead to vast, spacious rooms. From one wall hung the lasso, symbol of the binding ties of marriage. Nieves clutched a white glove in her left hand, her left arm at a ninety-degree angle. She stood next to Juan Luz, and both of them faced out.

Nieves's hair was short, in the style of the twenties, with soft, loose curls, not as she later wore it, in a bun, austere.

Juan Luz was handsome, with a full head of hair that on second glance seemed subject to thinning, if not local baldness. His hands were tightly clenched, hers were relaxed. They gazed forward, loving, bright-eyed, with hand-painted pink cheeks. They were sealed in time—a photograph on their happiest day.

One year later, Juan Luz was dead, Nieves was a widow, Ronelia was born, and Mercy and I were still in limbo. On a higher shelf, Nieves's closet was full of old phonograph records, "The Singing Nun," Agustín Lara, mementos of her teaching days, her work with children. Hers was a closet packed with scarves, new shoes, old photo albums, a chipped statue of San Martín de Porres, and tapes of the Living Bible and charismatic church revivals, as well as home movies of us as children standing by the Willow Tree.

VII

The closet floor is strewn with paper, boxes. When Mercy and I stand in there, with the Christ eyes, we have to be careful.

"Leave me alone! It's my turn!"

"Give me the Christ eyes, Rocío!"

"Oh, go lay down, baby."

"Don't pull that knob, Mother's gonna find out and get mad. You made me knock something over."

"Okay, okay, let me find the cord. There, see. That didn't take so long. Hey, Mercy, if you crouch down like this, it's better. That way, you feel darker."

I crouched in the closet wanting to know what it felt to be crucified, to carry the sins of the world on my shoulders. I knew I'd already earned my crown of thorns. I imagined the splinters, the wood.

"How did you find it, Rocío?" Mercy asked when I

finally told her about the Gray Room. "Do you think it has something to do with seeing the house's bones, its skeleton? I mean the wood, the house frame, the concrete slabs?"

"Remember that sliced-away mountain by the highway?" I said. "All my life I thought mountains were soft inside."

"You're kidding."

"Seeing that mountain changed my life! It was one of the five most important things that ever happened to me; the discovery of perspective in fourth grade was three."

"What are two, four, and five, Rocío?"

"I can't tell you that, Mercy."

"Tell me, tell me," she begged.

"God bless, do I have to tell you *everything*?"

"Look, I'll tell you about the Gray Room. Will you be quiet then? I'm in the hallway closet. I see Grandpa's death mask wrapped in white satin. I see the box of paper dolls we got for Christmas. I see your crown from elementary school when you were Bazaar Queen. Why did you cry? I wouldn't have cried, but then I wasn't Queen. I move aside the belt cord from Mother's green bathrobe. I uncover the box of Christmas cards. I move the old rubber rain shoes and clear plastic raincoats. I make room for myself and step inside. I glide past everybody. I am far away now, past the color and the noise, past the cloth shadows. I am past everyone. Alone. Alone without noise. I don't need to turn on the light."

"Oh, but Rocío, aren't you afraid of the dark?" Mercy said at last, trying on the crown of thorns and then putting them on her side of the bed. "Aren't you afraid of the Christ eyes?"

"Not of the Christ eyes," I answered, "but the brown animals scare me, and I don't want to be afraid."

"Tell me about the Blue Room," she said after a long pause. "It sounds *so* beautiful."

"It is," I said, lying down to rest on the bed, not bothering to tell her she was on my side again. "It's a wonderful enormous room and it's blue. But you know, the other day I went in there and it was all white and the floor was like dry ice."

"You mean it changes?" Mercy looked at me with surprise. "Tell me about it before it changed," she said drowsily.

"The Blue Room is my favorite room. It's the most magnificent, incredible room you'd ever hope to see, Mercy. It has a round ceiling that goes up forever. It's so big that I have to fly back and forth to get around. It's a beautiful room and it's mine. All mine!"

"Golly," Mercy said, yawning.

"Watch it! You almost made me turn over on the thorns. Put them up, would you?"

"Rocío, Rocío, if that's *your* room, *what's mine?*"

"I don't know, Mercy. Everybody has their *own* rooms, their *own* house."

"They do?" she said with a faraway voice.

"Gaaa, Mercy, do I have to tell you *everything?*"

Down the aisles of Woolworth's with my other self, Christmastime 1960. Three shopping days left, a dollar for each day, and all I had was my awkward youth and one question: "What can I buy for you this Christmas, Mother?"

The cellophane cannot conceal the rich colors of my dreams, the midnight blue bottles of Evening in Paris, the gift package I so long to receive myself. The deep, pungent smell is sealed in silver and blue. Twinkling stars surround me as I ponder the inevitable. But first, "Just looking."

The lady at the counter has brows like a man's, fiercer than a man's. She is someone like Mrs. Limón who lives down the street, with her brown eyebrows shaped like fish and her large fleshy smell.

I stand while the saleslady, Mrs. Limón Jr., slides a serpentine hand along those clear glass compartments of ice-cold adulthood, bringing into the light pale lipsticks in pink and white, and small compact circles of Angel Face powder, translucent as the sun. No salves, ointments, or cremes this time—

"Just looking." My hungry lips and young girl's face contemplate a cloudy potential self.

Please hurry, I haven't time to linger. My mother and sister are somewhere in this store, this circus of objects, searching for opiates, rickrack. I am wonderstruck by the colors behind the glass, by my image in the mirror, by the smell of this blue midnight time. It is as strong as the scent of woman, as far away as a Paris full of lights.

The partitions in the case speak of care. "Now, don't you touch," the eyebrows say. Color me Rosy Red, Angel Pink, Hot Rose, Dusty Brown, and Heavenly Blue. My eyes are brown. But in the mirror they are Velvet Black, Torrid Blue, and Nile Green.

I take out my Christmas gift list, crossing out Father. Mother takes care of him, house shoes and a tie. She signs the card, "We love you, Daddy."

My sister? I don't know. Mother comes first. Perfume is what I want. Limón looks at me, probably thinks to herself: "What help is there?"

I wonder myself as I stare at my flat chest, the limp darts on my blouse. Young, make—me—beautiful girl, flesh out my dreams of a dark, perfumed lady with loves. What promise is there for three-dollar realities?

Mother gave me a wallet with Christ's picture on it to give to my sister. He is a Jesus anyone would love. He is so handsome with his long, curly beard, thick brown hair, his deep-set eyes that stare out. He was painted by someone named Sallman, who perhaps saw him in a vision or dream. Everything is removed from me. Paris. Christ. Men become flesh. Everything is removed from me, my awkward limbs, uncertain dreams.

I am afraid to be seen looking at myself in the mirror, in my uniform of navy blue, with my white blouse and navy beanie, the center button of the beanie gone, torn off. I look down at my bobby socks, the only pair I own. I wash them every morning, dry them on the heater, wear them dripping wet to school. I wore them then, in that after-school time of if only this and how to that.

I have decided to buy the gift package of Evening in Paris cologne and bath water for my mother.

"I'll take this please," my voice falters. I don't remember how to speak. I am afraid, my clothes all wrong. Can't you cover me up? Shape my doubts, pluck my nervousness away, mask the fear, and seal the lips with hope for self? Dynamite Red, of course.

The package lies heavily in my hands. I must not drop it. Oh, what a joyful treasure! This is the nicest gift I have ever given Mother. I know she will like it, I know she will. Scent of Mother: those lilies she loves in our front yard. Tabu no longer her only recourse.

The Paris of my mother's dreams momentarily fused with mine. They were one and the same, a child's dreams of happiness, but more. Glory. We revel in it, rich and powdered queens, no worrying about money or any man who goes away, leaving us perfumed, alone.

I am on the edge of that vast, compartmentalized sea, looking across islands of objects, most of them man-made. I give the stranger waves of green.

"Here's your change."

Mother is the only one I can buy a gift for this year. I'm sorry, all of you, my friends. No one expects a gift from a child, except other children.

"Where's my gift?" they say, and so you look in your room, in your drawers, for something that is not used, valuable. I forgot about the Jesus wallet. And I can slip in a School Day's picture. (I don't know what happened to me that day. I thought I looked so good. I put my hair over my ears so they wouldn't stick out, but they did, and so did the hair.)

There is a voice at the edge of this world. It is not the sour one's; she's turned away, shriveled up. The cash register has registered me. The voice calls: "Let's go, Mother's ready," and "What do you have in that package?"

Daylight darkens into dreams.

Most of the gifts under the tree are from Mother's students. We take turns passing them out—this is for you and this one and this one, too. Oh, and this is for *me*! The pile in front of Mother grows. Her usual gifts are uncovered: a book of Life Savers, Avon perfume in a white plastic vase, some green Thinking of You stationery, several cotton handkerchiefs flowered with roses, and a package of divinity, we'll all enjoy that. Most of these gifts will go into the gift box, so next year I'll have something to give *my* teacher. But for now, they are relegated to a temporary space on the rug, to be covered by the falling needles of our dying tree.

That particular tree lasted into February. It was with great reluctance that it was dispatched into oblivion, which in this case was the irrigation ditch behind the house. The longest tree was flocked; we did it ourselves. The flocking hung from dried bushes and clung to the yellow winter grass, all the snow that would be seen *that* year. Summer and dust were the only real seasons I knew growing up. The dry brown grass announced the end of one season, the beginning of another.

Only farmers and the young, who live dependent upon change, understand what it is to know the continual flowering of life, however subtle.

In childhood, our bright faces eagerly sought the reflections of our imagined selves in the boxes of fabricated well-being found at Woolworth's. Most of us become mannequins, tucked into life's compartments. We take on roles, illusions with which to arm ourselves against the ever-changing mirrors of age. Eventually we see the edge of this material world, with its objects and playthings. But then we were stuck! Heavenly Blue with a tinge of sweet cotton candy, little rosettes of illusion. And mine were the proudest, most sustained. They were founded upon hopes.

I recall the smell of our kitchen in those days of Christmas. There was a chicken in the oven, our Christmas "turkey." Empanadas de calabaza, indented and grooved into symmetry, lay in what might have been the turkey tin, alongside bizcochos laid out by my mother's holiday hands.

Most likely there was someone around to help us then, a maid from México, a friend like Ninfa, who told us stories about the overly curious mouse who fell into the stew and was later eaten for his impudence. Or maybe it was Emilia, who showed me the round, not rectangular worlds of tortillas and how you turn–push down–turn–keep turning, the rolling pin her instrument of grace.

There was a familiarity of shelves and counters where one perched along blue linoleum expanses and stared into the blocked universe of Emilia's cutting board. Her squat, heavy hands, her Savior's hands—she once saved me from sure death on the Tilt-A-Whirl—kneaded circular balls of inanimate masa into future life.

Oftentimes Emilia would lean over, and with her flour-covered hands would search the airways for her favorite station, XELO.

"Ay, qué lejos estoy del cielo donde he nacido," she sang, as from my mother's room floated the sound of my favorite Christmas carol, "We Three Kings," sung so effortlessly by Perry Como.

It is enveloped in blue, this time of the past.

The shelf closest to the kitchen table was one of Mother's miscellaneous shelves, her where-to-put-something-that-I-don't-know-what-to-do-with space. These four large areas contained many parts of my mother's life. The first held old dishes, cups and saucers, crystal plates with a thin, slightly greasy layer of moist dust, a bowl in the shape of a duck, its bright orange beak and blue eyes opened in constant surprise.

Near the back was a small statue of the Infant Jesus of Prague, in a long, red robe, his head awry but held in place with a wadded, previously chewed stick of Juicy Fruit gum, his arms extended in benevolent greeting. This memento was the gift of some distressed Anglo woman who had spent several days with us, searching for her Filipino husband who was working in the cotton fields. She was one of the many who passed through our youthful lives, as servers or served.

"Can I help you?" Mother said, and so she did, and they in turn left part of themselves with us. There was a constant stream of faces, but it was those few that I remembered, like the lady with the unsteady Infant Jesus of Prague who stayed in my room and cried to herself while I slept on the couch.

The other shelves were similar to the first, with old dishes, broken wedding gifts, small bud vases, and an occasional statuette. Amongst the clutter were other objects: a twined now dried collection of palms from previous Palm Sundays, a small paper sack of biznaga, my mother's favorite cactus candy from Juárez, a cone of piloncillo, a half-empty box of Fig Newtons, a few votive candles left over from last year's luminarias, and in the corner, far from prying eyes, an ashtray filled with old cigarette butts left by my father on his last visit. These inanimate objects assumed a banal ordinariness in full daylight, and yet their internal life danced in a darkness of significance and could never be understood by the casual observer.

Each object on those shelves had its smell and touch and taste. In those days of Sugar, it was the piloncillo I gravitated toward, as I secretly chipped away rich amber edges of the hardened dark brown sugar and devoured them with delight.

The cigarette butts I lifted and pondered, and once tried to smoke one in a long solitary afternoon in the backyard, near the garbage can, in that blind space that allowed concealment, freedom.

The dishes were tokens of inaccessible and indecipherable emotions known only to my Mother. As I stared into those crystalline plates embossed with streams of invisible words, how little I understood the sublime fluctuations of my Mother's heart.

The time came around for Mother to open the dark blue gift that I had so carefully wrapped in white tissue paper. It seemed to me that this Christmas I had, at last, found the perfect gift for her. The anticipation I felt uprooted any commonplace joy I might have felt upon receiving any gifts that stood before me in "my" pile.

My sister's face fell as I handed the bright white package to Mother. I quickly gave my sister a smaller unboxed gift. The Jesus wallet. Mother had signaled Ninfa to start gathering up wrapping paper and to put the bows in a plastic bag. I asked sheepishly, "Aren't you going to open your gift?" for as far as I was concerned, there was only one. "This one, it's from me."

"Yes, oh yes," she said, and stooped over to pick up several stray piles of gift-wrapping paper.

Later it seemed to me that perhaps Mother had thought the Evening in Paris had been given to her by one of her students. I even imagined that she'd been disappointed in my gift. I couldn't understand why. Maybe she actually preferred Tabu.

The shimmering star-filled box ended up under the tree, along with the handkerchiefs and the Life Savers. For a long time it stayed there, unopened, unused. The Avon perfume somehow found its way into Mother's room.

Those nights it was my custom to sit in the darkness of the living room near the tree and watch the lights. The luminarias hazily burned their way into the black-blue night. As usual, I felt unfulfilled, empty, without the right words, gifts, feelings for those whose lives crowded around me and who called themselves my family. How removed I felt, as far away as Paris, a city that I felt was no longer glamorous or ageless or full of illusion.

Much later, when I was older and found myself in Paris, it was the lost little girl who understood so much of its reality. It was the person of the inappropriate gifts who followed hunchbacked old women on winding metal stairways into grayed, murky expanses of sky.

It was a Paris of balding, hennaed heads and odors of sausage exuded by men with polished black umbrella handles that I knew as intimately as the painted, unreal worlds of the postcard Tour Eiffels that said "Wish You Were Here," and "Sending Love Across the Miles."

But that Paris of lights and magic does still exist. I have seen it, inside the haunting, starless nights. And this is what I felt when I sat in the deep embracing darkness of that special tree, the one that stayed with us the longest.

Going back is going forward. It is better to give than to receive. All the familiar boring lessons are, after all, true.

The Infant Jesus of Prague with his gummed head eventually came to watch over those two ill-fated bottles of Evening in Paris perfume. The candy changed shelves, was consumed, replaced, consumed. The wedding gifts were covered in plastic. Time was sectioned off, divided like the little glass containers at Woolworth's, each holding some illusion.

Previous intensity became a stale wash of growing up, without the standing back to choose.

I'll take this color here, that perfume there. . . . That one. Evening in Paris. Dark blue bottle, liquid manifestation of so much hope, of long European nights, of voices mingling in the darkened streets, calling out: "Remember me, remember me."

The following Christmas Mother gave me the Jesus wallet. She'd forgotten that the year before I'd given it to my sister, who in turn had given it to her for the gift box.

What need had Mother of perfume on those dusty playgrounds?

What need had I of wallets?

That Sallman did a good job. You know the picture, don't you? He is a Christ that anyone could love, with his long brown curls and beard—his deep-set eyes staring out. . . .

When I was a young girl, I conjured images from the white walls of my father's old study room. Faces leapt out from the plaster's twists and turns. These imaginings consumed the lazy summer afternoons. I was supposed to have been napping, but inevitably I wandered back to the faces in the walls, to the vast ruminations of my adolescent self.

What did it mean to be a woman? To be beautiful? Complete? Was beauty a physical or spiritual thing? Was it strength of emotion, resolve, a willingness to love? What was it, then, that made women lovely?

The images in the wall receded and then like bright dancing beams of light burst into my consciousness. I thought of Eloisa, Diana, and Josie. One by one their faces broke out to the wall's textured surface and into my dreams to become living flesh and blood.

In my mind I was back in Texas, a place I always apologized for. It was a place removed from normal experience, the farthest spot away from my hoped-for reality. As part of that unvoiced obedience to parental rule, my sister and I spent a portion of each summer with my mother's Texas relatives.

One of our favorite pastimes was to sell wildflowers in a makeshift shop. We picked them in a nearby vacant lot sectioned off by a chain-link fence that spiraled downward into an uncultivated field. We stuck the clumps of stray flowers in the cinder-block slots of my aunt's stone wall.

Occasionally, the grayed and moving form of an old man materialized, alongside those of several angry dogs. Yet our flower industry was never totally shut down.

The summer days passed this way, one upon another, in the ritual of the flower picking. No one knew of this flower industry, no one ever bought these flowers, but it mattered little to my sister and me. Each day we would set out our display, pricing and haggling between ourselves, then sitting down to wait for customers. It didn't matter that our shop lay at the end of a dead-end street, or that the summer heat wilted customer and flower alike.

These days passed from the early-morning obscurities of waking up, dressing, eating breakfast, and wandering about the house to heightened afternoons of rummaging through my grandmother's shelves. They held warm, softened objects, handkerchiefs and embroidered limpiadores with pale stitched roses on a fading background of days: lunes, martes, miércoles. In the corners, wrapped in filmy plastic bags, were peinetas still holding tufts of strong, dark hair.

Later, I would go through my aunt's chest of drawers. Although it was never spoken of, I knew my aunt had cancer and was dying. In her drawers were pieces of paper with obscure names, felt bookmarkers, and small hardbound books with either God or Daisy in the title.

I found once, on a bookshelf, a collection of fairy tales, all previously unread, that still haunt me today. In one story, several dogs, with eyes like huge, wild saucers, guarded a magic spellbound castle. In another, a mermaid whose fins magically turned into feet learned to walk on land, beside an unfeeling lover who did not see the pain each bloody footstep cost her.

In the days of those stories, there were mud pies and one summer, an infestation of worms. The worms oozed their way into my aunt's stone house, crawling from the marble floors onto the walls, and hung there, seeking shade in the torpid summer afternoon. We used all our ingenuity to kill them. Death by stomping. Death by insecticide. Death by scalding.

One of my dying aunt's bookshelves held *The Incredible Shrinking Man,* a book that I have regretted reading. That summer I spent long hours imagining my disappearance in that ever-fearful darkness children know so well.

In the evenings we slept outside, for it was always too hot in the house. Our adopted family consisted of my aunt, whose joys were watermelon and books, my silent and morose uncle, my two strange cousins, my grandmother, Mother, Mercy, and me.

Each of us had our separate cots. Mine hugged the wall near the side of the house that faced the long hot highway that reached farther and deeper into Texas. It was a bit set off from the others. Lying down, I could see the low mountains on the horizon to my left, and in front, the shadow of the straw roof that housed the makeshift barbecue pit that was used on fiestas, holy days. In the silent summer darkness, the imaginary aromatic memories of cabrito floated to me, along with the sound of phantom voices, haunted guitars.

As the hot, steaming nights grew longer, everyone would gravitate outside to the back of the house. Each cot would be surrounded by watermelon seeds, the moist remnants of that evening ritual. My mother and aunt sat on cots facing each other, eating gleefully and laughing about some past episode in the life of their favorite uncle, the incomparable Acorcinio, who as a drunk was prone to tears and sober was someone to be reckoned with.

My uncle would be napping inside, facedown on his single bed. My two cousins were nowhere to be found. Mercy, busy with her watermelon, dangled her legs between the metal grating of the cot's side. Curled up in my sheet, I would stare up into the sky. Somewhere not so far away, a lone and anxious coyote called to the moon.

One day we rode into a small nearby town to visit relatives: a thin old lady with a fifty-year-old retarded daughter and a talkative middle-aged man whose father had once been my grandmother's beau.

It was then I came to know Eloisa, a local girl, the daughter of a family friend. Her aunt wore men's shirts and pants and bound her breasts with rags. One day I found out that Eloisa's mother and aunt (half men to me) were relatives! This made Eloisa, too, part of my mother's family. Most of them were a queer, unbalanced lot.

Eloisa was sixteen, already a woman. It was she who instigated our many walks around the town, a place of well-kept churches, with large, wide streets. But poverty was always just around the corner. My grandmother and her sister, Eutilia, were proof of this: one of them spoke English and was postmistress of the town, the other was hunchbacked, private, only spoke Spanish, and lived next door in a tiny wooden shack.

Up Main Street we would go, past the record shop, with its few 45s of Tiny Morrie and Dion, near the five-and-dime, past the Paisano Hotel, where the cast of the movie *Giant* had stayed, the short but lovely Elizabeth Taylor and James Dean, who had allegedly wooed my teenage cousin, Zenaida. Up we'd go to the courthouse, and around the block, into familiar and dear streets. Our walks were without time or sense. They were talking walks, stopping walks. How I admired Eloisa! How grateful I was for her allowing me into her magical woman's world. Eloisa and I were bright girls, mature girls, and always trailing behind us was my little sister, Mercy.

Later, after the nightly watermelon, I would fall asleep under the stars thinking of Eloisa. She was Venus, I was a shooting star. The two of us were really one. We were beautiful girls, bright beautiful girls spitting out watermelon seeds. We were coyotes calling out to the moon.

That summer I carried Eloisa around with me—her image a holy card, revered, immutable, an unnamed virgin. That is, until the Jeff Chandler movie at the Pasatiempo Theater.

Sitting in the darkness of the theater, front row, little sister in tow, I saw, on my way to the candy counter, none other than Eloisa. She was sitting with friends. Smoke rose from their lips. My heart sank. I was sick with nicotine, faint with its smell. I wandered back to my seat. Jeff Chandler, tanned idol, was suddenly a blanched earthworm. A nervous bull terrier yapped on the screen, and I sank down in my seat, pretzel-like, sick to my heart.

Eloisa smoked cigarettes!

When I had recovered from the shock, I stole my way back to the rear of the theater, where Eloisa sat, chortling and braying like a rude goat. She was not alone, she was with a man, and he had his paws across her shoulder.

I crawled back to my seat again, faint with disappointment. I don't remember the rest of the movie. I barely remember that Jeff Chandler was in it. I do remember that we didn't take many other shortcuts through the sculptured lawns of the First Presbyterian Church. Fall was coming. It was time to go home to New Mexico, my father, the sun.

To me, Texas signified strange days, querulous wanderings, bloody fairy tales, hot, moon-filled nights, earthworms, and unbought flowers. Texas was women to me: my aunt dying of cancer, my grandmother's hunchbacked sister, and Eloisa. All laughing, laughing. Summer was a yapping dog and a dream of becoming ever smaller.

Diana was another of those young women who suddenly appeared in my life. Diana was lovely and apparently guileless. She did not smoke. She did have a boyfriend. One day I spoke of saving myself for marriage, and Diana said that yes, she too, was saved.

Her boyfriend, Rubén, was a childhood sweetheart. They used to play together. He was steadfast and loyal, dark like Diana, and very smart. Anyone who loved Diana must surely be smart. Diana had manners. Sí Señora this and Sí Señora that. Nice. Nice, and with the ugliest sister this side of Texas. Her sister had flat feet, spider veins, droopy nalgas, and empty, legaña-ridden eyes.

New Mexico is as unlike Texas as the moon is unlike the sun.

Diana was the personification of all that her sister was not. She was, like her namesake, the huntress in her clear, animal grace. She was simply Diana, fresh, bright-eyed, hopeful, and kind. Perhaps too kind. But this weakness of her spirit did not manifest itself at first. Diana was my older sister when my older sister married and was continually birthing nieces and nephews for me. She was my confidante, someone I looked up to, respected, loved. Unlike her Texas counterpart, Diana was first and foremost a friend who would never betray, no never. Nor could she see the possibility of betrayal. In this assumption of hers and mine lies all the tragedy of all young womankind.

What was it then, that made Diana beautiful to me? I thought as I sat in the kitchen, facing her small, strong back. Her body darted across the room to pick up a stray cup, now a plate. The steaming hot water rose and frosted the windows, fogging the view of the cotton fields, the world beyond.

Diana's beauty came from a certain peacefulness, not her own, but mine, that lived and breathed when I was with her. To me, the dirty kitchen, the smell of warmed food, the humid moistness of steamy windows, all this was peace to me. Peace and love. That crowded kitchen always and forever was a reminder of Diana, who filled the space with her high, bright laughter.

When Diana laughed, she laughed at all life, at all dirt. Her laughter echoed through the room, and then the house. It crossed the fields and fogged all consciousness. All memory became as the water beads on the glass panes: small, wet, persistent, clinging pools.

Who was this woman? Briefly my mother's assistant, our solitary sister for so short a while.

Beauty is silent, does not speak. For when Diana spoke, she was not beautiful but naive, a little girl. She had a thick accent, knew little English, talked a little too loudly. Once when my friends came over for my birthday party, everyone was awed by her beauty, until we started playing ball and she yelled shrilly, "Throw me the ball to me!" Later my friends teased me about Diana's speech and I couldn't say anything to defend her.

In observing Diana, I observed myself. I wanted physical beauty, and yet I wanted to speak well, to be understood.

Eloisa, my earlier womanly model, had walked far into the stars, and then gotten lost in the sickening odor of cigarette smoke at the back of the crowded movie theater. Diana now, too, was lost to me as a model. Her music was confused, jangled, unsure. Her thoughts were half syllables, monosyllabic utterings of someone dependent upon the repetitious motions of work, the body and its order.

The fields outside the northern window opened up to other views, not of the sky, but of the fecund movements of the sweet earth's turning.

Again that laugh . . .

It wasn't until later that I heard again of Diana. She and Rubén were running a home cleaning service, D and R Janitorial Service. They had two sons. Rubén left her periodically to live with her former maid. One Sunday I saw her in church, mustached, wrinkled, with frightened eyes. The dog-faced sister was nearby. She was now beautiful and happily married. La comadre Clara, Diana's mother, an old spotted monkey in ribbons, said to me, "Ay, Rocío, aquí está la Diana! Diana! You remember her?"

Mother of God, Diana, the goddess, I thought, she's gone. . . .

Diana's face vanished into the concrete walls.

I closed my eyes. I imagined I was on La Calle del Encuentro going past the Márquez house. In my waking life I never got inside.

Josie lived there with her mother and her sister, Mary Alice. It was the same street my uncle lived on, the uncle who had a swimming pool. As a result, the street was revered in my mind. It was probably the widest in town. It was broad and empty, lapping into the houses of my uncle, the house of the transient (later to become the house of my cousin with the gold toothpick), and the house of the Romanos.

Every day, paunchy, balding Mr. Romano would dash outside in his sleeveless T-shirt and khaki shorts to get the evening paper and move the hose to the rosebushes. His was a house where tragedy lived and bloomed, like the bloodred roses in the front yard. He lost one of his children to suicide; the other was run over by a truck. His was a house, even in those early days, that echoed pain.

Up from there, on the left, across the street, was the home of the druggist. And next to it was the Márquez home, a white temple of obscure shadow, a house of women.

As children we drove past the Márquez home either on the way to school or back. I was filled with curiosity about the house and the people who lived there. The front lawn was neat, sculptured. It was apparent that no one spent much time in the yard. Too public. There was also a barricaded backyard. I tried to catch a glimpse behind the curtains or beyond the white brick wall. I don't remember whether I saw anything or not. Shadows of dark-haired women, perhaps, with half-completed gestures, mouths open, in half-light. It was in this state of remembrance that I saw the form of Josie's mother. Mrs. Márquez was a tensely correct and aristocratic woman who was too beautiful for her own good. She spoke a Spanish of clipped sexual tension with no release. Her hair was dark brown, not black, and it framed her dark, smoldering face.

And what of Mr. Márquez? Who was he? I never saw or even heard of him, and yet, someone built that dream house. Who?

Josie's sister, Mary Alice, was a little replica of Mrs. Márquez. She was my older sister's age, and I was not close enough to that world of teenage concerns to be able to say I knew her well. The impression I had of Mary Alice was of a lovely, dark-haired girl eating a hamburger in an ad in the 1956 Bulldog annual. She is munching happily with three or four friends, one a fellow with neat, greased-backed hair, while two or three girls lean on a counter, in long, pleated skirts, tight, revealing sweaters, and penny loafers. Perhaps this is not the real Mary Alice; maybe it was she that sits at the Florist's Shop, ordering a boutonniere, or she that thumbs the racks in the Smart Shop ad.

While Mary Alice remained an indecipherable mystery to me, as did the striking mother, it was Josie, the youngest Márquez, who was the subject of my unrelenting speculations about the mysteries of womanhood. I began my questioning with Eloisa, continued it with Diana, and was left still unsure and trembling about my own uncertain womanhood when I began to study the memorable, but very short, Josie Márquez.

Josie had the finely chiseled Márquez nose and full, pouty lips. Her teeth were white and even, like a small rodent's. Her eyes were the eyes of a playful and willful child. Her hands were long and slender, the nails painted red. Josie's hair was black, and she wore it in curls trained around her unusually long neck, which would have been prized by Japanese men. Josie had a generously full and high bust. It seemed she always managed to push it out farther and fuller than even those women with pointy, elongated breasts. As she grew older she took advantage of this asset. The necklines plunged, the dresses accentuated her ripe cleavage, the whiteness of her skin. From the side of her blouse I could see the curve of her pale, lovely breasts.

I saw Josie at the parties held in the neighborhood by groups of older teenagers and college students who would gather to dance in someone's parents' TV room or vacant rental. It was here that my cousins perfected the cha-cha steps, fanning out, then touching hands, and then cha-cha-ing back to their sophisticated partners.

At one of these parties my cousin Lorraine, only a year older than I, surpassed my babyness and found her way into the light of young adulthood. It was at these parties that the embodiment of all my womanly hopes, Josie Márquez, one-two-cha-cha-cha-ed her way into eternity. I stood in the darkness near the punch bowl, humming a litany of displacement.

Josie always seemed to be either entering or exiting these

parties. Her voice rang out greetings, burbled and chortled hellos and good-byes. Her black spike heels clicked and turned and danced their way out the door with tall, handsome strangers, sophomores and juniors at the state university who belonged to the Newman Center and were majoring in mechanical engineering and who loved to dance.

Josie's closest friend was our neighbor, Barbara, who Ronelia says is doomed to her mother's face. Her face, alas, was Texas stock, with a nose that would reach the horizontal boundaries of that beloved state.

In those days Barbara was the person who was always going from a tint to a rinse, from blond to brunette, from streak to different-colored streak. She was a tall and gangly woman who "did the best" with what she had, and somehow managed to effect an attractiveness from her almost horsey features. Later she married the man of everyone's dreams, perhaps her own. His name was Derrick, and he was brought up around Amarillo, a tall, handsome, and rugged ex-farmer, the epitome of masculine beauty to everyone who saw him. Barbara was the same woman who slept in her makeup. This was the same woman who wore tiny, tight curlers and a fuzzy, pink bathrobe and who cried on leaving her mother's house for her own, even though it had a swimming pool.

"Good-bye, Mama, I'll miss you."

To see Barbara and Josie was to see two very different body types and souls. Yet, it seemed to me that they had the closest womanly ties between them. Both were charming, vibrant, effusive bird creatures, trapped in lovely, shiny cages. They did not have the spirit of Eloisa, the gentleness of Diana, but they seemed so happy to sing! Theirs was the blinding, powerful song of women, sisters!

For most of us, choice is an external sorting of the world that forces us to confront our own uncertain internal emptiness. Who was I, then, to chose as role model? Eloisa, Diana, Josie, or Barbara?

None seemed quite womanly enough. Something seemed to be lacking in each of them—the same thing that was lacking in me, whatever it was. I became the ever more solitary observer of my changing womanhood. I was jealous of those women who had effected the change from girlhood to womanhood with ease. I was at the far end of the crystal punch bowl. I heard the faraway music, saw all the colors and the lights, and yet, I was unable to join the dance.

Eloisa's fulfillment in the flesh, coupled with Diana's shattered dreams, somehow intertwined with Josie's pattering, pounding rhythm. I was caught in Josie's dance, and when I spun loose of all my illusionary partners, students from State, majoring in life, I felt a vague, disconcerting lack of joy.

The joy had once been in the quiet walks, in the long summer afternoons when Diana was at the sink, laughing, telling stories in a broken language that can never be repeated. Josie chortles hello. Hello.

In the hazy half-sleep of my daily nap, the plaster walls revealed a new face. Behind all the work of growing up, I caught a glimpse of someone strong, full of great beauty, power, clear words and acts. The woman's white face was reflected in the fierce midday sun, with the bright intensity of loving eyes.

Who was that woman?

Myself.

★   ★   ★

I thought about *loving* women. Their beauty and their doubts. Their sure sweet clarity. Their unfathomable depths. Their flesh and souls aligned in mystery.

I got up, looked in the mirror, and thought of Ronelia, my older sister, who was always the older woman to me. It was she whom I monitored last. It was she whose life I inspected, absorbed into my own.

It was my sister's pores, her postures that were my teachers, her flesh, with and without clothes, that was my awakening, and her face that was the mirror image of my growing older. To see her was to see my mother and my grandmother and now myself.

I recalled Ronelia standing with her back to me, in underwear. How I marveled at her flesh, her scars. The charting of my sister's body was of great interest to me. I saw her large, brown eyes, her sensual lips (always too big for her) soften and swell into dark beauty. How helpless she was, how dear! It was she who grabbed me when I was fearful that I would never be able to choose, to make up my mind. One time she and another young married woman cornered me, picked over me, my skin. Her friend hissed at me to toe the womanly line.

"For godsakes, Rocío, stand up straight, and do *something* about your hair!"

I felt hopelessly doomed to vagueness. Everything seemed undefined: my hair, my skin, my teeth, my soul.

I'm incapable of making decisions, Ronelia, I thought. Leave me alone. Why are you attacking me? Get on with your babies and your fetid errands! But instead of crying out, I sat forward, bit my lip, and allowed those two young matrons to attempt a transformation of me, an indecisive girl with bumpy skin.

We never spoke of growing older, or seeing others grow older, with any sense of peace. It was a subject that was taboo, a topic like Death.

How could I imagine that all the bright young girls, the Jennies and the Mary Lous, the Eloisas and the Dianas and the Josies, with their solid B-cups, their tangle of lovers, their popularity, and their sureness would one day become as passing shadows on the white canvases of late-afternoon dreams?

When I lay in the solemn shade of my father's study, I thought of myself, of Eloisa, of all women. The thoughts swirled around like the rusty blades of our swamp cooler. Each lugubrious revolution brought freshness, change. Shifting through the many thoughts, I heard voices in the afternoon silence.

Perhaps someday when I grew older, I thought, maybe then I could recollect and recount the real significance of things in a past as elusive as clouds passing.

The turning plaster waves revealed my sisters, my mother, my cousins, my friends, their nude forms, half-dressed, hanging out, lumpish, lovely, unaware of self, in rest rooms, in dressing rooms, in the many stalls and theaters of this life.

I was the monitor of women's going forth. Behind the mirror, eyes half-closed, I saw myself, the cloud princess.

Looking in the mirror, I saw my root beer eyes (my mother's phrase) in front as I monitored my flesh.

I addressed my body, the faint incandescent loveliness of its earliest, but not dearest, blooming. Could I imagine the me of myself at age twenty-one and thirty-one and so on?

I turned the mirror to the light. The loveliness of women sprang from depthless recesses. It was a chord. A reverberation. The echo of sound. A feeling. A twinge. And then an ache.

Always there is an echo of the young girl in the oldest of women, in small wrists encased in bulky flesh, in the brightest of eyes surrounded by wrinkles.

There is a beauty in hands tumultuous with veins, in my grandmother's flesh that I touched as a child, flesh that did not fall, but persisted in its patterning. Her skin was oiled old cloth, with twists and folds and dark blue waves of veins on a cracked sea of flesh.

On my dream canvas my grandmother pats her hands and says, "Someday, someday, Rocío, you'll get this way."

Women. Women with firm, sure flesh. In dreams. Let them go. They were reflections of light, a child's imaginings at naptime, patterns on plaster walls, where shapes emerged, then receded into hazy swirls before the closing of an eye. They were clouds, soft bright hopes. Just as quickly as they were formed, they dissolved into vast cloud pillows. Their vague outlines touched the earth and then moved on. . . .

★　　★　　★

Sharp patterns on the walls and ceilings, faces in the plastered waves, all those women, all of them, they rise, then fall. Girls, girls, the bright beautiful girls, with white faces and white voices, they call out. They are shooting stars, spitting seeds. They are music. The echo of sound. The wind.

Somewhere, very far away . . . a lone coyote calls out to the moon, her Mother.

THE LAST OF THE MENU GIRLS

NAME: Rocío Esquibel

AGE: Seventeen

PREVIOUS EXPERIENCE WITH THE SICK AND DYING:
   My great-aunt Eutilia

PRESENT EMPLOYMENT: Work-study aide at
   Altavista Memorial Hospital

I never wanted to be a nurse. My mother's aunt died in our house, seventy-seven years old and crying in her metal crib: "Put a pillow on the floor. I can jump," she cried. "Go on, let me jump. I want to get away from here, far away."

Eutilia's mattress was covered with chipped, clothlike sheaves of yellowed plastic. She wet herself, was a small child—undependable, helpless. She was an old lady with a broken hip, dying without having gotten down from that rented bed. Her blankets were sewn by my mother: corduroy patches, bright yellows, blues, and greens. And still she wanted to jump!

"Turn her over, turn her over, turn her, wait a minute, wait—turn. . . ."

Eutilia faced the wall. It was plastered white. The foamed concrete turnings of some workman's trowel revealed day-dreams: people's faces, white clouds, phantom pianos slowly playing half-lost melodies. "Las Mañanitas," "Cielito Lindo," songs formulated in expectation, dissolved into confusion. Eutilia's faces blurred, far-off tunes faded into the white walls, into jagged, broken waves.

I never wanted to be a nurse. All that gore and blood and grief. I was not as squeamish as my sister Mercy, who could not stand to put her hands into a sinkful of dirty dishes filled with floating food—wet bread, stringy vegetables, and bits of softened meat. Still, I didn't like the touch, the smells. How could I?

When I touched my mother's feet, I looked away, held my nose with one hand, the other with fingers laced along her toes, pulling and popping them into place.

"It really helps my arthritis, baby—you don't know. Pull my toes. I'll give you a dollar. Find my girdle, and I'll give you two. Ouch. Ouch. Not so hard. There, that's good. Look at my feet. You see the veins? Look at them. Aren't they ugly? And up here, look where I had the operations, . . . ugly, they stripped them and still they hurt me."

She rubbed her battered flesh wistfully, placed a delicate and lovely hand on her right thigh. Mother said proudly, truthfully, "I still have lovely thighs."

PREVIOUS EXPERIENCE WITH THE SICK AND DYING:
Let me think. . . .

Great-aunt Eutilia came to live with us one summer, and seven months later she died in my father's old study. The walls were lined with books—whatever answers were there—unread.

Great-aunt Eutilia smelled like the mercilessly sick. At first, a vague, softened aroma of tiredness and spilled food. And later, the blown evacuations of the dying: gas, putrefaction, and fetid lucidity. Her body poured out long held-back odors. She wet her diapers and sheets and knocked over medicines and glasses of tepid water, leaving a sickening odor in the air.

When I was thirteen, I danced around her bed, naked, smiling, jubilant. It was an exultant adolescent dance for my dying aunt. It was a necessary primitive dance, a full-moon offering that led me slithering into her room with breasts naked and oily.

There was no one home but me. . . .

The dance led me to her room, my father's refuge, those halcyon days now that he had divorced us. All that remained of his were dusty books, cast-iron bookends, reminders of the spaces he filled.

Down the steps I leaped into Eutilia's faded and foggy consciousness, where I whirled and sang: "I am your flesh and my mother's flesh and you are . . . you are . . ."

Eutilia stared at me. I turned away.

I danced around Eutilia's bed. I hugged the screen door, my breasts indented by the mesh wire. In the darkness Eutilia moaned, my body wet, her body dry, both of us full of prayers.

Could I have absolved her dying with my life? Could I have lessened her agony with my spirit-filled dance in the deepest darkness?

The blue fan stirred, then whipped the solid air nonstop; little razors slicing through consciousness and prodding the sick and dying woman. Her whitened eyes stared out as she screeched: "Ay! Ay! Let me jump, put a pillow. I want to go away. . . . Let me. . . . Let me . . ."

All requests were silenced. Eutilia rested in her tattered hospital gown, having shredded it to pieces. She was surrounded by little white strips of raveled cloth. She stared at the ceiling, having played the piano far into the night. She listened to sounds coming from around the back of her head. Just listened. Just looked. Shredded the rented gown. Shredded it. When the lady of the house returned and asked how she was, meaning does Eutilia breathe, her babysitter, Toño, answered, "Fine."

Christ on his crucifix! He'd never gone into the room to check on her. Later, when they found her, Toño cried, his cousin laughed. They hugged each other, then cried, then laughed, then cried.

Eutilia's fingers never rested. They played beautiful tunes. She was a little girl in tatters in her metal bed with sideboards that went up and down, up and down. . . .

The young girls danced, they played, they danced, they filled out forms.

PREVIOUS EMPLOYMENT: None

There was always a first job, as there was the first summer of the very first boyfriend. That was the summer of our first swamp cooler. The heat bore down and congealed sweat. It made rivulets trace the body's meridians, and before it stopped, it was wiped away but never quite dismissed.

On the tops of the neighbors' houses, old swamp coolers, with their jerky, grating and droning moans, strained to ease the southern implacabilities. Whrr whrr whrr.

Regino Suárez climbed up and down the roof, first forgetting his hammer and then the cooler filter. His boy, Eleiterio, stood at the bottom of the steps that led to the sundeck and squinted dumbly at the blazing sun. For several days Regino tramped above my dark purple bedroom. I had shut the curtains to both father and son and rested in violet contemplation of my first boyfriend.

If Eutilia could have read a book, it would have been the Bible, or maybe her novena to the Santo Niño de Atocha, he was her boy. . . .

PREVIOUS EXPERIENCE WITH THE SICK AND DYING:

This question reminds me of a story my mother told me about a very old woman, doña Mercedes, who was dying of cancer. Doña Mercedes lived with her daughter, Corina, who was my mother's friend.

The old woman lay in bed, day after day, moaning softly, not actually crying out loud, but whimpering in a sad, hopeless way.

"Don't move me," she begged when her daughter tried to change the sheets or bathe her. Every day this ordeal of maintenance became worse. It was a painful thing and full of dread for the old woman, the once fastidious and upright doña Mercedes. She had been an imposing lady, with a head full of rich dark hair. Her ancestors were from Spain.

★   ★   ★

"You mustn't move me, Corina," doña Mercedes pleaded, "never, please. Leave me alone, mi'jita." And so the daughter acquiesced.

Cleaning around her tortured flesh and delicately wiping where they could, my mother and Corina attended to doña Mercedes. She died in the daytime, as she had wished.

When the young women went to lift the old lady from her deathbed, they struggled to pull her from the sheets; and when finally they turned her on her side, they saw huge gaping holes in her back where the cancer had eaten through her flesh. The sheets were stained, the bedsores lost in a red wash of bloody pus. Doña Mercedes's cancer had eaten its way through her back and onto those sheets.

"Don't move me, please don't move me!" she had cried.

The two young women stuffed piles of shredded disinfected rags soaked in Lysol into doña Mercedes's chest cavity. Filling it, horrified, with cloths over their mouths, they said prayers for the dead.

Everyone remembered doña Mercedes as tall and straight and very Spanish.

PRESENT EMPLOYMENT: Work-study aide at Altavista Memorial Hospital

I never wanted to be a nurse. Never. The smells. The pain. What was I to do, then, working in a hospital, in that place of white women, whiter men with square faces? I had no skills. Once in the seventh grade I got a penmanship award. Swirling *R*s in boredom, the ABCs ad infinitum. Instead of dipping chocolate cones at the Dairy Queen next door to the hospital, I found myself, a frightened girl in a black skirt and white blouse, standing near the stairwell to the cafeteria.

I stared up at a painting of a dark-haired woman in a stiff nurse's cap and gray tunic, tending to men in old-fashioned service uniforms. There was a beauty in that woman's face, whoever she was. I saw myself in her, helping all of mankind, absolving all my own sick, my own dying, especially relatives, all of them so far away, removed. I never wanted to be like Great-aunt Eutilia, or doña Mercedes with the holes in her back, or my mother, her scarred legs, her whitened thighs.

Mr. Smith

Mr. Smith sat at his desk surrounded by requisition forms. He looked up at me with glassy eyes like filmy paperweights.

MOTHER OF GOD, MR. SMITH WAS A WALL-EYED HUNCHBACK!

"Mr. Smith, I'm Rocío Esquibel, the work-study student from the university, and I was sent down here to talk to you about my job."

"Down here, down here." He laughed, as if it were a private joke. "Oh yes, you must be the new girl. Menus," he mumbled. "Now, just have a seat, and we'll see what we can do. Would you like some iced tea?"

It was nine o'clock in the morning, too early for tea.

"No, well, yes, that would be nice."

"It's good tea, everyone likes it. Here, I'll get you some."

Mr. Smith got up, more hunchbacked than I'd imagined. He tiptoed out of the room whispering, "Tea, got to get this girl some tea."

There was a bit of the gruesome golem in him, a bit of the twisted spider in the dark. Was I to work for this gnome? I wanted to rescue souls, not play attendant to this crippled, dried-up specimen, this cartilaginous insect with his misshapen head and eyes that peered out at me like the marbled eyes of statues in a museum. History preserves its freaks. God, was my job to do the same? No, never!

I faced Dietary Awards, Degrees in Food Management, menus for Lo Salt and Fluids; the word Jell-O leapt out at every turn. I touched the walls. They were moist, never having seen the light.

In my dreams, Mr. Smith was encased in green Jell-O; his formaldehyde breath reminded me of other smells—decaying dead things: my great-aunt Eutilia, biology class in high school, my friend, Dolores Casaus.

Each of us held a tray with a dead frog pinned in place, served to us by a tall stooped-shouldered Viking turned farmer, our biology teacher, Mr. Franke, pink-eyed, half-blind. Dolores and I cut into the chest cavity and explored that small universe of dead cold fibers. Dolores stopped at the frog's stomach, then squeezed out its last meal, a green mash, spinach-colored viscous fluid—that was all that remained of that miniaturized, unresponding organ.

Before Eutilia died, she ate a little, mostly drank juice through bent and dripping hospital straws. The straws littered the floor where she'd knocked them over in her wild frenzy to escape.

"Diooooooooooooo!" she cried in that shrill voice. "Dios mío, Diosito, por favor. Ay, I won't tell your Mamá, just help me get away. . . . Diosito de mi vida . . . Diosito de mi corazón . . . agua, agua . . . por favor, por favor . . ."

Mr. Smith returned with my iced tea.

"Sugar?"

Sugar, yes, sugar. Lots of it. Was I to spend all summer in this smelly cage? What was I to do? And for whom? I had no business here. It was summertime and my life stretched out magically in front of me: there was my boyfriend, my freedom. Senior year had been the happiest in my life. Was it to change?

"Anytime you want to come down and get a glass of tea, you go right ahead. We always have it on hand. Everyone likes my tea," he said with pride.

"About the job?" I asked.

Mr. Smith handed me a pile of green forms. They were menus.

In the center of the menu was listed the day of the week, and to the left and coming down in neat order were the three meals, breakfast, lunch, and dinner. Each menu had various choices for each meal.

LUNCH:

❏ Salisbury steak

❏ Fish sticks

❏ Enchiladas

❏ Rice almandine

❏ Mashed potatoes and gravy

❏ Macaroni and cheese

❏ Broccoli and onions

DRINKS	DESSERT
❑ Coffee	❑ Jell-O
❑ Tea	❑ Carrot cake
❑ 7-Up	❑ Ice cream, vanilla
❑ Other	

"Here you see a menu for Friday, listing the three meals. Let's take lunch. You have a choice of Salisbury steak, enchiladas, they're really good, Trini makes them. She's been working for me for twenty years. Her son, George Jr., works for me, too, probably his kids one day."

At this possibility, Mr. Smith laughed to himself.

"Oh, and fish sticks. You a . . ."

"Our Lady of the Holy Scapular."

"Sometimes I'll get a menu with a thank-you note written on the side, 'Thanks for the liver, it was real good,' or 'I haven't had rice pudding since I was a boy.' Makes me feel good to know we've made our patients happy."

Mr. Smith paused, reflecting on the positive aspects of his job.

"Mind you, these menus are only for people on regular diets, not everybody, but a lot of people. I take care of the other special diets, that doesn't concern you. I have a girl working for me now, Arlene Rutschman. You know . . ."

My mind raced forward, backward. Arlene Rutschman, the Arlene from Holy Scapular, Arlene of the soft voice, the limp hands, the affected mannerisms, the plain, too goodly face, Arlene, president of Our Lady's Sodality, in her white and navy blue beanie, her bobby socks and horn-rimmed glasses, the Arlene of the school dances with her perpetual escort, Bennie Lara, the toothy better-than-no-date date, the Arlene of the high grades, the muscular yet in-turned legs, the curly unattractive hair, *that* Arlene, the dud?

"Yes, I know her."

"Good!"

"We went to school together."

"Wonderful!"

"She works here?"

"Oh, she's a nice girl. She'll help you, show you what to do, how to distribute the menus."

"Distribute the menus?"

"Now you just sit there, drink your tea, and tell me about yourself."

This was the first of many conversations with Mr. Smith, the hunchbacked dietician, a man who was never anything but kind to me.

"Hey," he said proudly, "these are my kids. Norma and Bardwell. Norma's in junior high, majoring in boys, and Bardwell is graduating from the Military Institute."

"Bardwell. That's an unusual name," I said as I stared at a series of five-by-sevens on Mr. Smith's desk.

"Bardwell, well, that was my father's name. Bardwell B. Smith. The Bard, they called him!"

At this, he chuckled to himself, myopically recalling his father, tracing with his strange eyes patterns of living flesh and bone.

"He used to recite."

The children looked fairly normal. Norma was slight, with a broad toothy smile. Bardwell, or Bobby, as he was called, was not unhandsome in his uniform, if it weren't for one ragged, splayed ear that slightly cupped forward, as if listening to something.

Mrs. Smith's image was nowhere in sight. "Camera shy," he said. To the left of Mr. Smith's desk hung a plastic gold-framed prayer beginning with the words "Oh Lord of Pots and Pans." To the left, near a dried-out watercooler, was a sign, BLESS THIS MESS.

Over the weeks I began to know something of Mr. Smith's convoluted life, its anchorings. His wife and children came to life, and Mr. Smith acquired a name: Marion, and a vague disconcerting sexuality. It was upsetting for me to imagine him fathering Norma and Bardwell. I stared into the framed glossies full of disbelief. Who was Mrs. Smith? What was she like?

Eutilia never had any children. She'd been married to José Esparza, a good man, a handsome man. They ran a store in Agua Tibia. They prospered, until one day, early in the morning, about 3 A.M., several men from El Otro Lado called out to them in the house.

"Don José, wake up! We need to buy supplies."

Eutilia was afraid, said, "No, José, don't let them in."

"Woman," he told her, "what are we here for?"

And she said, "But at this hour, José? At this hour?"

Don José let them into the store. The two men came in carrying two sacks, one that was empty, and another they said was full of money. They went through the store, picking out hats, clothing, tins of corned beef, and stuffing them into the empty sack.

"So many things, José, *too* many many things!"

"Oh no," one man replied, "we have the money. Don't you trust us, José?"

"Como no, compadre," he replied easily.

"We need the goods. Don't be afraid, compadre."

"Too many things, too many things," Eutilia sighed, huddled in the darkness in her robe. She was a small woman, with the body of a little girl. Eutilia looked at José, and it was then that they both knew. When the two men had loaded up, they turned to don José, took out a gun, which was hidden in a sack, and said, "So sorry, compadre, but you know. . . . Stay there, don't follow us."

Eutilia hugged the darkness, not saying anything for the longest time. José was a handsome man, but dumb.

The village children made fun of José Esparza, laughed at him and pinned notes and pieces of paper to his pants. "Tonto, tonto" and "I am a fool." He never saw these notes, wondered why they laughed.

"I've brought you a gift, a bag of rocks." Fathers have said that to their children. Except don José Esparza. He had no children, despite his looks.

"At times a monkey can do better than a prince," la comadre Lucaya used to say to anyone who would listen.

The bodies of patients twisted and moaned and cried out and cursed, but for the two of us in that basement world, all was quiet save for the occasional clinking of an iced tea glass and the sporadic sound of Mr. Smith clearing his throat.

"There's no hurry," Mr. Smith would say. "Now, you just take your time. Always in a hurry. A young person like you."

Arlene Rutschman

"You're so lucky you can speak Spanish," Arlene intoned. She stood on tiptoe, held her breath, then knocked gently on the patient's door. No sound. A swifter knock. "I can never remember what a turnip is," she said.

"Whatjawant?" a voice bellowed.

"I'm the menu girl; can I take your order?"

Arlene's high tremulous little-girl's voice trailed off.

"Good morning, Mr. Samaniego! What'll it be? No, it's not today you leave, tomorrow, after lunch. Your wife is coming to get you. So, what'll it be for your third-to-the-last meal? Now, we got poached or fried eggs. Poached. P-o-a-c-h-e-d. That's like a little hard in the middle and a little soft on the outside. Firm. No, not like scrambled. Different. Okay, you want scrambled. Juice? We got grape or orange. You like grape? Two grape. And some coffee, black."

A tall Anglo man, gaunt and yellowed like an old newspaper, his eyes rubbed black like an old raccoon's, ranged the hallway. He talked quietly to himself and smoked numbers of cigarettes as he weaved between attendants with half-filled urinals and lugubrious IVs. He reminded me of my father's friends, angular Anglos in their late fifties, men with names like Bud or Earl, men who owned garages or steak houses, men with firm hairy arms, clear blue eyes, and tattoos from the war.

"That's Mr. Ellis, 206. Jaundice," Arlene whispered.

"Oh," I said, curiously contemptuous and nervous at the same time, unhappy and reeling from the phrase, "I'm the menu girl!"

How'd I ever manage to get such a dumb job? At least the

candy stripers wore a cute uniform, and they got to do fun things like deliver flowers and candy.

"Here comes the wife."

"Mr. Ellis's wife?" I said, with concern.

"No, Mr. Samaniego's wife, Donelda." Arlene pointed to a wizened and giggly old woman who was sneaking by the information desk, past the silver-haired volunteer, several squirmy grandchildren in tow. Visiting hours began at 2 P.M., but Donelda Samaniego had come early to beat the rush. From the hallway, Arlene and I heard loud smacks, much joking, and general merriment. The room smelled of tamales.

"Old Mr. Phillips in 304, that's the medical floor, he gets his cath at eleven, so don't ask him about his menu then. It upsets his stomach."

Mrs. Daniels in 210 told Arlene weakly, "Honey, yes, you, honey, who's the other girl? Who is she? You'll just have to come back later. I don't feel good. I'm a dying woman, can't you see that?" When we came back an hour later, Mrs. Daniels was asleep, snoring loudly.

Mrs. Gustafson, a sad, wet-eyed, well-dressed woman in her late sixties, dismissed us from the shade of drawn curtains as her husband, G. P. "Gus" Gustafson, the judge, took long and fitful naps, only to wake up again, then go back to sleep, beginning once more his inexorable round of disappearance.

"Yesterday I weighed myself in the hall and I'm getting fat," Arlene whined. "Oh, and you're so thin."

"The hips," I said, "the hips."

"You know, you remind me of the painting," Arlene said, thoughtfully.

"Which?"

"Not which, who. The one in the stairwell. Florence Nightingale, she looks like you."

"That's who that is!"

"The eyes."

"The eyes?"

"And the hair."

"And the hair?"

"The eyes and the hair."

"The eyes and the hair? Maybe the hair, but not the eyes."

"Yes."

"I don't think so."

"Oh yes! Every time I look at it."

"Me?"

Arlene and I sat talking in the cafeteria at our table, which later was to become *my* table. It faced the dining room. From that vantage point, I could see everything and not be seen.

We talked, two friends, almost, if only she weren't so, so, little girlish with her ribbons. Arlene was still dating Bennie and was majoring in either home ec or biology. They seemed the same in my mind: menus and frogs. Loathsome, unpleasant things.

It was there, in the coolness of the cafeteria, in that respite from the green forms, at our special table, drinking tea, laughing with Arlene, that I, still shy, still judgmental, still wondering and still afraid, under the influence of caffeine, decided to stick it out. I would not quit the job.

"How's Mr. Prieto in 200?"

"He left yesterday, but he'll be coming back. He's dying."

"Did you see old Mr. Carter? They strapped him to the wheelchair finally."

"It was about time. He kept falling over."

"Mrs. Domínguez went to bland."

"She was doing so well."

"You think so? She couldn't hardly chew. She kept choking."

"And that grouch, what's her name, the head nurse, Stevens in 214 . . ."

"She's the head nurse? I didn't know that—god, I filled out her menu for her. . . . She was sleeping and I . . . no wonder she was mad. How would I know she was the head nurse?"

"It's okay. She's going home or coming back, I can't remember which. Esperanza González is gonna be in charge."

"She was real mad."

"Forget it, it's okay."

"The woman will never forgive me. I'll lose my job." I sighed.

I walked home past the Dairy Queen. It took five minutes at the most. I stopped midway at the ditch's edge, where the earth rose and where there was a concrete embankment where you could sit. To some this was the quiet place, where neighborhood lovers met on summer nights to kiss, and where older couples paused between their evening walks to rest. It was also the talking place, where all the neighborhood kids discussed life while eating hot fudge sundaes with nuts. The bench was large; four could sit on it comfortably. It faced an open field in the middle of which stood a huge apricot tree. Lastly, the bench was a stopping place, the "throne" we called it. We took off hot shoes and dipped our cramped feet into the cool ditch water, as we sat facing the southern sun at the quiet talking place, at our throne, not thinking anything, eyes closed, but sun. The great red velvet sun.

One night I dreamed of food, wading through hallways of food inside some dark, evil stomach. My boyfriend waved to me from the ditch's bank. I sat on the throne, ran alongside his car, a blue Ford, in which he sat, on clear plastic seat covers, with that hungry Church-of-Christ smile of his. He drove away, and when he returned, the car was small and I was too big to get inside.

Eutilia stirred. She was tired. She did not recognize anyone. I danced around the bed, crossed myself, en el nombre del padre, del hijo, del espíritu santo, crossed forehead, chin, and breast, begged for forgiveness, even as I danced.

And on waking, I remembered. *Nabos.* Turnips. But of course.

It seemed right to be working in a hospital, to be helping people, and yet: why was I only a menu girl? Once a menu was completed, another would take its place and the next day another. It was a never-ending round of food and more food. I thought of Judge Gustafson.

When Arlene took a short vacation to the Luray Caverns, I became the official menu girl. That week was the happiest of my entire summer.

That was the week I fell in love.

Elizabeth Rainey

Elizabeth Rainey, Room 240, was in for a D and C. I didn't know what a D and C was, but I knew it was mysterious, and to me, of course, this meant it had to do with sex. Elizabeth Rainey was propped up with many pillows, a soft blue homemade quilt at the foot of her bed. Her cheeks were flushed, her red lips quivering. She looked fragile, and yet her face showed a harsh bitterness. She wore a cream-colored gown on which her loose hair fell about her like a cape. She was a beautiful woman, full-bodied, with the translucent beauty certain women have in the midst of sorrow—clear, unadorned.

She cried out to me rudely, as if I had personally offended her. "What do you want? Can't you see I want to be alone. Now close the door and go away! Go away!"

"I'm here to get your menu," I said softly. I could not bring myself to say, "I'm the menu girl."

"Go away, go away. I don't want anything. I don't want to eat. Close the door!"

Elizabeth Rainey drew her face away from me and turned to the wall. From the depths of her being a small inarticulate cry escaped, "Oooooh."

I ran out, frightened by her pain, yet excited somehow. She was so beautiful and so alone. I wanted in my little-girl's way to hold her, hold her tight, and in my woman's way to never feel her pain, ever, whatever it was.

"Go away, go away," she said, her mouth trembling with pain, "go away!"

How many people yelled at me that summer, have yelled since then, countless people, of all ages, sick people, really sick people, dying people, people who were well and were still tied to their needs for privacy and space, affronted by these constant impositions from, of all people, the menu girl!

"Move on, would you? Go away! Leave me alone!"

And yet, of everyone who told me to go away, it was this woman in her solitary anguish who touched me the most deeply. How could I, age seventeen, not knowing love, how could I presume to reach out to this young woman in her sorrow, touch her and say, "I know, I understand."

Instead, I shrank back into myself and trembled behind the door. I never went back into her room. How could I? It was too terrible a vision, for in her I saw myself, all life, all suffering. What I saw both chilled and burned me. I stood a long time in that darkened doorway, confused in the presence of human pain. I wanted to reach out. . . . I wanted to. . . . I wanted to. . . . But *how*?

As long as I live I will carry Elizabeth Rainey's image with me: she is propped up in a cream-colored gown, her hair fanning pillows in a room full of sweet, acrid, overspent flowers. Oh, I may have been that summer girl, but yes, I knew, I understood. I would have danced for her, Eutilia, had I dared.

Dolores Casaus

Dolores, of the frog entrails episode, was now a nurse's aide on the surgical floor, changing sheets, giving enemas, and taking rectal temperatures. It was she who taught me how to take blood pressure, wrapping the cuff around the arm, counting the seconds, and then multiplying beats. As a friend, she was rude, impudent, delightful; as an aide, most dedicated. One day for an experiment, with me as a guinea pig, she took the blood pressure of my right leg. That day I hobbled around the hospital, the leg cramped and weak. In high school Dolores had been my double, my confidante, and the best Ouija board partner I ever had. When we set our fingers to the board, the dial raced and spun, flinging out letters— notes from the long dead. Together we contacted La Llorona and would have unraveled *that* mystery if Sister Esperidiana hadn't caught us in the religion room during lunchtime communing with that distressed spirit who had so much to tell.

Dolores was engaged. She had a hope chest. She wasn't going to college because she had to work, and her two sisters-in-law, the nurses González and González—Esperanza, male, and Bertha, female—were her supervisors.

As a favor to Dolores, González the Elder, Esperanza, would often give her a leftover tray of "regular" food, the intended having checked out or moved on to other resting grounds. Usually I'd have gone home after the ritualistic glass of tea, but one day, out of boredom perhaps, most likely out of curiosity, I hung around the surgical floor talking to Dolores, my only friend in the entire hospital. I clung to her sense of wonder, her sense of the ludicrous, to her humor in the face of order, for even in that environment of restriction, I felt her still probing the whys and wherefores of science with immense childlike curiosity.

The day of the leftover meal found Dolores and me in the laundry room, sandwiched between bins of feces- and urine-stained sheets to be laundered. There were also dripping urinals waiting to be washed. Hunched over a tray of fried chicken, mashed potatoes and gravy, lima beans, and vanilla ice cream, we devoured crusty morsels of Mr. Smith's fried chicken breasts. The food was good. We fought over the ice cream. I resolved to try a few more meals before the summer ended, perhaps in a more pleasant atmosphere.

That day, I lingered at the hospital longer than usual. I helped Dolores with Francisca Pacheco, turning the old woman on her side as we fitted the sheets on the mattress.

"¡Cuidado, no me toquen!" she cried. When Dolores took her temperature rectally, I left the room, but returned just as quickly, ashamed of my timidity. I was always the passing menu girl, too afraid to linger, too unwilling to see, too busy with summer illusions.

Every day I raced to finish the daily menus, punching in my time card, greeting the beginning of what I considered to be my real day outside those long and smelly corridors where food and illness intermingled, leaving a sweet thick air of exasperation in my lungs. The "ooooh" of Elizabeth Rainey's anxious flesh.

The "ay, ay, ay" of Great-aunt Eutilia's phantom cries awaited me in my father's room. On the wall the portrait of his hero, Napoleon, hung, shielded by white sheets. The sun was too bright that summer for delicate, fading eyes, the heat too oppressive. The blue fan raced to bring freshness to that acrid tomb full of ghosts.

I walked home slowly, not stopping at the quiet place. Compadre Regino Suárez was on the roof. The cooler leaked. Impatient with Regino, his hearty wave, his habit of never finishing a job completely, I remembered that I'd forgotten my daily iced tea. The sun was hot. All I wanted was to rest in the cool darkness of my purple room.

The inside of the house smelled of burned food and lemons. My mother had left something on the stove again. To counteract the smell, she'd placed lemons all over the house. Lemons filled ashtrays and bowls; they lay solidly on tables and rested in hot corners. I looked in the direction of Eutilia's room. Quiet. She was sleeping. She'd been dead for years, but still the room was hers. She was sleeping peacefully. I smelled the cleansing bitterness of lemons.

Mrs. Daniels

When I entered rooms and saw sick, dying women in their forties, I always remembered room 210, Mrs. Daniels. She usually lay in bed, whimpering like a little dog, moaning to her husband, who always stood nearby, holding her hand, saying softly, "Now, Martha, Martha. The little girl only wants to get your order."

"Send her away, goddammit!"

On those days that Mr. Daniels was absent, Mrs. Daniels yelled for me to go away.

"Leave me alone. Can't you see I'm dying?" she would say. She looked toward the wall. She was pale, sick, near death, but somehow I knew—not really having imagined death without the dying, not having felt the outrage and the loathing—I knew and saw her outbursts for what they really were: deep hurt, profound distress. I saw her need to release them, fling them at others, dribbling pain/anguish/abuse, trickling away those torrential feelings of sorrow and hate and fear, letting them fall wherever they would, on whomever they might. I was her white wall. I was the whipping girl upon whom she spilled darkened ashes. She cried out obscenely to me, sending me reeling from her room—that room anxious with worms.

Who of us has not heard the angry choked words of crying people, listened, not wanted to hear, then shut our ears, said enough, I don't want to. Who has not seen the fearful tear-streamed faces, known the blank eyes and, like smiling thoughtless children, said, "I was in the next room, I couldn't help hearing, I heard, I saw, you didn't know, did you? I know."

We rolled up the pain, assigned it to a shelf, left it there, with a certain self-congratulatory sense of relief at our own good fortune as we looked the other way at the world's unfortunates, like Mrs. Daniels. For a while we were embarrassed to be alive. And soon, we forgot we had ever felt any discomfort.

Juan María the Nose

"Como se dice when was the last time you had a bowel movement?" Nurse Luciano asked. She was from Yonkers, a bright newlywed. Erminia, the ward secretary, a tall thin horsey woman with a postured Juárez hairdo of exaggerated sausage ringlets, replied through chapped lips, "Oh, who cares, he's sleeping."

"He's from Mexico, huh?" Luciano said with interest.

"An illegal alien," Rosario retorted. She was Erminia's sister, the hospital superintendent's secretary, with the look of a badly scarred bulldog. She'd stopped by to invite Erminia to join her for lunch.

"So where'd it happen?" Luciano asked.

"At the Guadalajara Bar on Main Street," Erminia answered, moistening her purple lips nervously. It was a habit of hers.

"Hey, I remember when we used to walk home from school. You remember, Rocío?" Dolores asked. "We'd try to throw each other through the swinging doors. It was real noisy in there."

"Father O'Kelley said drink was the defilement of men, and the undoing of staunch, God-fearing women," I said.

"Our father has one now and then," Rosario replied. "That doesn't mean anything. It's because he was one of those aliens."

"Those kind of problems are bad around here I heard," Luciano said. "People sneaking across the border and all."

"Hell, you don't know the half of it," Nurse González fired back as she came up to the desk where we all stood facing the hallway. "It's an epidemic."

"I don't know, my mother always had maids, and they were all real nice except the one who stole her wedding rings. We had to track her all the way to Piedras Negras, and even then she wouldn't give them up," Erminia interjected.

"Still, it doesn't seem human the way they're treated at times."

"Some of them, they ain't human," González said thickly.

"He was drunk, he wasn't full aware," Luciano countered.

"Full aware my ass," retorted Esperanza González angrily. "He had enough money to buy booze. If that's not aware, I don't know what aware is. Ain't my goddamn fault the bastard got into a fight and someone bit his nose off. Ain't *my* fault he's here and we gotta take care of him. Christ! If *that* isn't aware, I don't know what aware is!"

Esperanza González, whose name meant "hope," head surgical floor nurse, the short but highly respected Esperanza of no esperanzas, the Esperanza of the short-bobbed hair, the husky voice, the no-nonsense commands, Esperanza the future sister-in-law of Dolores, my only friend; Esperanza the dyke, who was later killed in a car accident on the way to work, said: "Now, get back to work all of you. We're just here to clean up the mess."

Later, when Esperanza was killed, my aunt said, "How nice. In the paper they called her lover her sister. How nice."

"Hey, Erminia, lunch?" asked Rosario. "You hungry?"

"Coming, Rosario," yelled Erminia from the back office, where she was getting her purse. "Coming!"

"God, I'm starving," Rosario said. "Can you hear my stomach?"

"Go check Mr. Carter's cath, Dolores, will you?" said Esperanza in a softer tone.

"Well, I don't know, I just don't know," Luciano pondered. "It doesn't seem human, does it? I mean how in the world could anyone in their right mind bite off another person's nose? How? You know, González, you're a tough rooster. If I didn't know you so well already, you'd scare the hell out of me. How long you been a nurse?"

"Too long, Luciano. Look, I ain't a new bride; that's liable to make a person soft. Me, I just clean up the mess. Luciano, what you know about people could be put on the head of a pin. You just leave these alien problems to those of us who were brought up around here and know what's going on. Me, I don't feel one bit sorry for that bastard," Esperanza said firmly. "Christ, Luciano, what do you expect? He don't espeak no Engleesh!"

"His name was Juan María Mejía," I ventured.

"The Nose," Nurse González said with cruelty.

Luciano laughed. Dolores went off to Mr. Carter's room, and Rosario chatted noisily with Erminia as they walked toward the cafeteria.

"Hey, Rosario," Luciano called out, "what happened to the rings?"

It was enchilada day. Trini was very busy.

Juan María the Nose slept in the hallway; all of the other beds were filled. His hospital gown was awry, the gray sheet folded through sleep-deadened limbs. His hands were tightly clenched. The hospital screen barely concealed his twisted private sleep of legs akimbo, moist armpits and groin. It was a sleep of sleeping off, of hard drunken wanderings, with dreams of a bar, dreams of a fight. He slept the way little boys sleep, carelessly half exposed. I stared at him.

Esperanza complained and muttered under her breath, railing at all the Anglo sons of bitches and all the lousy wetbacks, at everyone, male and female, goddamn them all and their messes. Esperanza was dark and squat, pura india, tortured by her very face. Briskly, she ordered Dolores and now me around. I had graduated overnight, as if in a hazy dream, to assistant, but unofficial, ward secretary.

I stared across the hallway at Juan María the Nose. He faced the wall, a dangling IV at the foot of the bed. Esperanza González, R.N., looked at me.

"Well, and who are you?"

"I'm the menu, I mean, I *was* the menu . . ." I stammered. "I'm helping Erminia."

"So get me some cigarettes. Camels. I'll pay you back tomorrow when I get paid."

Yes, it was really González, male, who ran the hospital.

Arlene returned from the Luray Caverns with a stalactite charm bracelet for me. She announced to Mr. Smith and me that she'd gotten a job with an insurance company.

"I'll miss you, Rocío."

"I'll miss you, too, Arlene." God knows it was the truth. I'd come to depend on her, our talks over tea. No one ever complimented me like she did.

"You never get angry, do you?" she said admiringly.

"Rarely," I said. But inside, I was always angry.

"What do you want to do, Rocío?"

"Want to do?"

"Yeah."

I want to be someone else, somewhere else, someone important and responsible and sexy. I want to be sexy.

"I don't know. I'm going to major in drama."

"You're sweet," she said. "Everyone likes you. It's your nature. You're the Florence Nightingale of Altavista Memorial Hospital, that's it!"

"Oh God, Arlene, I don't want to be a nurse, *ever!* I can't take the smells. No one in our family can stand smells."

"You look like that painting. I always did think it looked like you."

"You did?"

"Yeah."

"Come on, you're making me sick, Arlene."

"Everyone likes you."

"Well . . ."

"So keep in touch. I'll see you at the university."

"Home ec?"

"Biology."

We hugged.

The weeks progressed. My hours at the hospital grew. I was allowed to check in patients, to take their blood pressure and temperature. I flipped through the patients' charts, memorizing names, room numbers, types of diet. I fingered the doctors' reports with reverence. Perhaps someday I would begin to write in them as Erminia did: "2:15 P.M., Mrs. Daniels, pulse normal, temp normal. Dr. Blasse checked patient, treatment on schedule, medication given to quiet patient."

One day I received a call at the ward desk. It was Mr. Smith.

"Miss Esquibel? Rocío? This is Mr. Smith, you know, down in the cafeteria?"

"Yes, Mr. Smith! How are you? Is there anything I can do? Are you getting the menus okay? I'm leaving them on top of your desk."

"I've been talking to Nurse González, surgical; she says they need you there full-time to fill in and could I do without you."

"Oh, I can do both jobs; it doesn't take that long, Mr. Smith."

"No, we're going by a new system. Rather, it's the old system. The aides will take the menu orders like they used to before Arlene came. So, you come down and see me, Rocío, have a glass of iced tea. I never see you anymore since you moved up in the world. Yeah, I guess you're the last of the menu girls."

The summer passed. June, July, August, my birth month. There were hurried admissions, feverish errands, quick notes jotted in the doctors' charts. I began to work Saturdays. In my eagerness to "advance" I had unwittingly created more work for myself, work I really wasn't skilled to do.

My heart reached out to every person, dragged itself through the hallways with the patients, cried when they did, laughed when they did. I had no business in the job.

I was too emotional.

Now when I walked into a room I knew the patient's history, the cause of illness. I began to study individual cases with great attention, turning to a copy of *The Family Physician,* which had its place among my father's old books in his abandoned study.

Gone were the idle hours of sitting in the cafeteria, leisurely drinking iced tea; gone were the removed reflections of the outsider.

My walks home were measured, pensive. I hid in my room those long hot nights, nights full of wrestling, injured dreams. Nothing seemed enough.

Before I knew it, it was the end of August, that autumnal time of setting out.

My new life was about to begin. I had made the awesome leap into myself that steamy summer of illness and dread—confronting at every turn the flesh, its lingering cries. "Ay, ay, ay, ay. ¡Canta y no llores! Porque cantando se alegran, Cielito Lindo, los corazones . . ."

The thin little voice of an old woman sang from one of the back rooms. She pumped the gold pedals with fast, furious, and fervent feet. She smiled to the wall, its faces, she danced on the ceiling.

Let me jump.

"Good-bye, Dolores, it was fun."

"I'll miss you, Rocío! But you know, gotta save some money. I'll get back to school someday."

"What's wrong, Erminia? You mad?" I asked.

"I thought you were going to stay and help me out here on the floor."

"Goddamn right!" complained Esperanza González. "Someone told me this was your last day, so why didn't you tell me? What'd I train you for, so you could leave us? To go to school? What for? So you can get those damned food stamps? It's a disgrace all those wetbacks and healthy college students are getting our hard-earned tax money. Makes me sick. Christ!" Esperanza shook her head with disgust.

"Hey, Erminia, you tell Rosario good-bye for me and Mrs. Luciano, too," I said.

"Yeah, okay. They'll be here tomorrow," she answered tonelessly. I wanted to believe she was sad.

"I gotta say good-bye to Mr. Smith," I said as I moved away.

"Make him come up and get some sun." González snickered. "Hell no, better not. He might get sunstroke and who'd fix my fried chicken?"

I climbed down the stairs to the basement, past the cafeteria, past my special table, and into Mr. Smith's office, where he sat, adding numbers.

"Miss Esquibel, Rocío!"

"This is my last day, Mr. Smith. I wanted to come down and thank you. I'm sorry about . . ."

"Oh no, it worked out all right. It's nothing."

Did I see, from the corner of my eye, a set of Friday's menus he himself was tabulating—Salisbury steak, macaroni and cheese. . . .

"We'll miss you, Rocío. You were an excellent menu girl."

"It's been a wonderful summer."

"Do you want some iced tea?"

"No, I really don't have the time."

"I'll get . . ."

"No, thank you, Mr. Smith, I *really* have to go, but thanks. It's *really* good tea."

I extended my hand, and for the first time, we touched. Mr. Smith's eyes seemed fogged, distracted. He stood up and hobbled closer to my side. I took his grave cold hand, shook it softly, and turned to the moist walls.

Eutilia's voice echoed in the small room. Good-bye. Good-bye. And let me jump.

When I closed the door, I saw him in front of me, framed in paper, the darkness of that quiet room. Bless this mess.

I turned away from the faces, the voices, now gone: Father O'Kelley; Elizabeth Rainey; Mrs. Luciano; Arlene Rutschman; Mrs. Daniels; Juan María the Nose; Mr. Samaniego and Donelda, his wife; their grandchildren; Mr. Carter; Earl Ellis; Dolores Casaus; Erminia and her sister, the bulldog, Esperanza González; Francisca Pacheco; Elweena Twinbaum, the silver-haired volunteer whose name I'd learned the week before I left Altavista Memorial. I'd made a list on a menu of all the people I'd worked with. To remember. It seemed right.

From the distance I heard Marion Smith's high voice: "Now, you come back and see us!"

Above the stairs the painting of Florence Nightingale stared solidly into weary soldiers' eyes. Her look encompassed all the great unspeakable sufferings of every war. I thought of Arlene typing insurance premiums.

Farther away, from behind and around my head, I heard the irregular but joyful strains of "Cielito Lindo," played on a phantom piano by a disembodied but now peaceful voice that sang with great quivering emotion: "De la sierra morena Cielito Lindo viene bajando. . . ."

Regino fixed the cooler. I started school. Later that year I was in a car accident. I crashed into a brick wall at a cemetery. I walked to Dolores's house, holding my bleeding face in my hands. Dolores and her father argued all the way to the hospital. I sat quietly in the backseat. It was a lovely morning. So clear. When I woke up, I was on the surgical floor. Everyone knew me. I had so many flowers in my room, I could hardly breathe. My older sister, Ronelia, thought I'd lost part of my nose in the accident, and she returned to the cemetery to look for it. It wasn't there.

Mr. Smith came to see me once. I started to cry.

"Oh no, no, no, no, now, don't do that, Rocío. You want some tea?"

No one took my menu order. I guess that system had finally died out. I ate the food, whatever it was, walked the hallways in my gray hospital gown slit in the back, railed at the well-being of others, cursed myself for being so stupid. I only wanted to be taken home, down the street, past the quiet-talking place, a block away, near the Dairy Queen, to the darkness of my purple room.

It was time.

PREVIOUS EMPLOYMENT: Altavista Memorial Hospital

SUPERVISORS: Mr. Marion Smith, Dietician, and Miss Esperanza González, R.N., Surgical Floor

DATES: June 1966 to August 1966

IN A FEW SENTENCES GIVE A BRIEF DESCRIPTION OF YOUR JOB: As Ward Secretary, I was responsible for . . . Let me think. . . .

SPACE   IS   A   SOLID

I

Kari Lee

"Space is a solid." Miss Esquibel explained this to us at the beginning of Drama Appreciation III class, but I'm not sure what she meant. Miss Esquibel told us to stand in the middle of the room, all of us kids, and "Pretend you are a molecule."

Arlin was cutting up and Miss E said, "Cut it out, just cut it. If you want to squirm, wait till you're a worm."

Everybody laughed, including me, even though I'm not sure what she meant by that. Anyway, Arlin was cutting up. Now that's pretty crazy 'cause he doesn't have any arms. All he has are these little stumps that stick out like the gills of a fish. When he gets excited, they flap up and down, up and down, like wings. My friend Deanna Werner has wings, too, but they're on her back. I call her the Chicken 'cause she's so skinny. When she has on a bathing suit, she makes her wings go pwaakk, up and down!

Arlin doesn't care about anything but mean boy things, like roughhousing and saying *hell* and *damn.* He'll start squawking and flapping around the room, bumping into people, and Miss E will say, "Good, Arlin, good! Molecules are like that, they hop and they pop and they bop!"

Everyone laughed but I think he was showing off because he didn't have any arms.

Mama told me, "You mean Arlin Threadgill is in your Drama Appreciation III class, why for land's sake, Kari Lee, he's a crippled boy! His mama was one of those that took that drug . . . Thalitomite, I think that's what they call it, causing that poor boy that horrible disfigurement for the rest of his born life. God Almighty, but ain't I glad you got no stumps like that, Kari Lee Wembley. No Wembley as far I can recollect had no disfigurement like that. And it was all on account of that Thalitomite! Drugs are dangerous, Kari Lee, look at your father's aunt, May Ethel, well, she started on some fancy prescribed drugs for her sciatica and wouldn't you know it, she started growing hair on her face like a man! No sir, Kari Lee, no Wembley can trace their disfigurements to drugs but your aunt May Ethel, and she was unsuspecting. Well, she stopped those drugs right then and there and endured her pain just like all the Wembleys done. Ain't right to pump your body with any enzodimes or mites, no thank you, ma'am. Listen to me, Kari Lee, now if God wants to send down his wrath on you, that's another thing altogether, why, he'll do it, now just don't you go pushing him."

If Mama stood in the middle of the room, she'd be a talking molecule. I was thinking about that when Miss E turned to me and said, "Kari Lee, what are you thinking?"

"Oh, I don't know."

"Quick, tell me, don't stop to think, Kari Lee. You're a molecule, remember?"

"I am?" I said, surprised.

"What does a molecule think?"

"What does a molecule think? Oh, about other molecules, I guess, Miss E." "Arlin! Don't you be whapping me with those chicken wings of yours," I almost said, but I stopped in time, and said, "Molecules don't think at all, Miss E, they just move."

"Like responding to stimuli," Arlin said.

"Good, Arlin, good!" Miss Michaelson said excitedly. She's the other Drama Appreciation III teacher, Miss E's boss, kinda.

"So molecules don't talk?" questioned Miss E. She was wearing a real neat velour top. She is so pretty and so friendly and so nice and so funny! Everyone likes her except Arlin, and well, he's a pill!

Mama says that sometimes people are pills, and that it's because they aren't normal, haven't got normal feelings and such, they're disfigured and all. They call attention to themselves just like Arlin. They prance and dance around just like little circus horses, showing how much they can do. Mama says, "Don't know what's wrong with Mrs. Threadgill, showing off Arlin all over town like he was normal. No, Kari Lee, it's all on account of that Thalitomite!"

Me, I won't have anything to do with that Arlin Threadgill, and it's not because he's a cripple. Arlin smells!

Arlin is a talking molecule and I'm a quiet molecule. Most of us molecules are quiet. We're doing just what molecules do, bumping into each other and saying excuse me and I'm sorry, did I hurt you, and then hitting someone else.

All except Ginita Wall. She's all balled up in a dark corner, not making a sound, just scrunched up with her head facing the floor, and her arms around her knees, like she can smell her crotch. Ginita always does something different.

If Miss E or Miss M says, "Pretend you're in an elevator and it's stuck between floors and the ceiling is coming down to you, closer and closer, and there's fifteen people in there, what would you do?" Well, anyone would scream. Not Ginita Wall. She'll climb through the trapdoor and save everybody. Or suppose you're supposed to be improvising you're at this bus station, and everything starts getting real dull or rowdy, which means that Arlin has started picking a fight with someone, Ginita will throw one of her epileptic fits right there in front of the ticket office. Anyone would notice *that*. So, wouldn't you know it, Arlin will be the one to put something in her mouth so she won't swallow her tongue or choke to death, and then he'll put a coat over her, and then he'll brag about it! Well, I guess that excepting for his wings, Arlin *could* become a doctor.

I guess there's all types of molecules. There's Arlin and me, and Ginita. Mama is like Arlin and Miss E is like Ginita and I'm like me. Only I wish I had a sister. Mama told me one day that it was too late for that foolishness. She didn't seem too interested in giving me a sister. She said that Daddy was too old, and she was too tired, and no Wembley woman begets after age forty, and here she went and upset the whole scheme, she, having me at age forty-two. "Well, it's just almost too much, Kari Lee," she always says, "me, Nita Wembley, getting ready to go into middle age with a youngster, something sacrilegious about it. Here me and your daddy tried for so long, and then I gave up and in my forty-second year, you come along, Kari Lee. Thank God you ain't disfigured! It sometimes happens in your later years. Not that I'm that old, Kari Lee! Oh, was Cloyd surprised! And what about me, nearly done with all that female business and looking forward to your daddy leaving me alone. Yes, it was a shock! I don't know, I wasn't right *prepared!*"

I don't know what Mama means when she says that; maybe she's just talking. She's got nobody to talk to except herself and me. Daddy doesn't talk much, all he does is work. Mama, too, she works and works, cleaning and renting apartments to people, helping Daddy with his plumbing business, and taking care of the house. She says *she's* the reason we live in Oak Hill Estates and are rich.

If space is a solid, then you can cut through it. Your arm is like a knife, and your body is a knife, too, and when you walk, not like normal, all slouched and lazy and kicking things, but as if you're aware and conscious and thinking, you're cutting through space.

My body is a knife.

"Trying walking like that," Miss E says. "All of you walk in a circle and imagine that you are cutting through space."

Oh, and then Arlin starts playing like he's got an imaginary sword in his imaginary hands and he's cutting space. Ginita looks at him and she keeps walking around the circle with a kinda strange but dignified walk like I've never seen her walk, like she's really cutting through space, and I can *almost* see what Miss E is talking about. Whether it's mud or ice or you're walking on glass or on a hot sidewalk in the summertime with bare feet, or even soft, green grass, keep thinking, "Space is a solid, space is a solid."

"Let's walk in molasses," Arlin says. Me and Ginita Wall

just look at each other and then at Arlin. Because of that Pill, with a capital *P*, everyone has to walk in molasses. Yuck. He *would* say molasses!

"What time is it?" Arlin says, 'cause he's bored. Oh, that Arlin, he's always so bored! If you're crippled, you get bored easier, that's what Mama says.

"Half an hour to go," says Miss M. She keeps watching the time too. Miss M looks bored; maybe she's waiting for that man who meets her after class. He's dark, probably from another country.

"If you're an American, marry an American. If you're colored, marry a colored. If you're Chinese, marry a Chinese," Mama says. "None of this other stuff, now. No Wembley has ever married anyone but they was from good old West Texas stock. That's the reason we ain't had no disfigurements in this family. Wembleys still Wembleys," Mama says. I wonder who Miss E's boyfriend is. She's *so* pretty!

"Lay down," Miss E says.

"Me lay down, no way in hell," says Arlin.

Arlin never stays after class to talk to anyone. His mama picks him up for his karate class, golly, and then he practices on us later!

"You ain't gonna get me to lay down like I was sick," says Arlin, "'cause I ain't sick and I ain't never been sick!"

"You aren't gonna get me," I correct.

Arlin stands there and flaps whiles me and Ginita lay down on the rug part of the room and giggle when our toes touch.

"Find a place that's all yours," says Miss E. "Spread your arms out."

Gosh, I wonder if hearing things like *that* makes Arlin feel like a worm; well, it's not *his* fault, it's his mama's, and that drug's.

"Spread out, relax, and breathe deeply," says Miss E with a hypnotizing voice. Arlin has *finally* laid down on the boys' side and is play-snoring.

"Find a place that's *yours,* belongs to *you,* and close your eyes."

"Aw, Miss Esquibel, do I have to?" Arlin whispers.

"Close your eyes, Arlin, breathe deeply and imagine you are as small as a molecule. You are becoming smaller and smaller and smaller, until you become so small you can enter your body, which is laying on the floor below you. You're at the top of the ceiling, so small and curious that you can go inside your body easily, like a molecule. You go through an orifice. . . ."

"Orifice!" shrieks Arlin.

"An eye or an ear or any other place you like," says Miss E.

Arlin snickers when somebody asks, "What's an orifice?" For a cripple, Arlin sure has a dirty mind.

"Now, wander inside and explore the space. What is it like?"

Arlin snickers again and then he farts! Everyone laughs and says, "EEEEeeeeeeeeyyyyywwwwwooooo!"

But Miss E says, "Now close your eyes and concentrate. C-O-N-C-E-N-T-R-A-T-E. Now, starting from where you are, go through your body, exploring it and seeing and feeling it, and smelling and touching. We're on a body journey this afternoon. No space is too small, too strange, or too unfamiliar to us. And if it is unfamiliar, or different, remember how it feels and smells and tastes. Is it dark? Crowded? How do you feel? Now, move on."

"Isn't it time to go home?" asks Arlin. "I got karate lessons," he mumbles.

Arlin starts kicking and my right leg is going to sleep and when I open my eyes, I can see Ginita so relaxed and happy like she *really* is on a body journey and having a wonderful time. I keep trying, I really do, but I just can't concentrate. I feel too itchy and nervous-like. It's Arlin that's bothering me, not Miss E, 'cause her voice is soft and soothing and she makes me think thoughts I've never thought before. But I just can't concentrate. Golly, I can smell Arlin's feet over here on the girls' side. I *really* am trying to think and remember and then move on inside my body. I guess that's what Miss E means. Concentrate. Concentrate, Kari Lee. I am. I am. Space is a solid. Space is a solid. Space is a solid.

II
Rocío

It was at this time that my hands started turning blue. I first noticed it going up an elevator to an opening-night cast party. Elevators give license to hysterical thoughts. Who hasn't imagined death in an elevator, crushed between floors, bodies piled up in broken heaps, strangers no longer.

Loudon, my boyfriend, stood solidly behind me in his navy blue, wool army store coat. His beard and shoulder-length hair flowed together in front of his kind, monastic face. Loudon was a radical in search of radicalism. He was going through the Machine, working on his M.F.A. in drama, that coveted crown of endurance. He was a large ex-football player gone to seed. He'd broken his leg the week before going to Vietnam with the marines, and he continued to limp in memory of his departed brothers, all of them blown up, blown away.

Loudon laid a puffy hand on my shoulder; his thick fingers caressed my thin neck thoughtlessly. It was the hand of the self-absorbed dreamer: squared, bitten-down.

I stared at the opening between the cushioned elevator doors.

"Aren't these pads used in lock-up tanks, Loudon, padded rooms for persons with psychological problems?"

Only the other day I tried on a straitjacket, my first fitting, in the costume shop. I'd been folding tights all morning in the tiny back room where we kept all the hats and tights and belts and underwear. I'd brought a footstool from the large front room where Solly Mathison was cutting a pattern for himself.

"Hey, Solly, I'm going to the back room to fold tights and straighten up back there. Call me if Mrs. Larsen comes up."

"So all right," Solly said, absorbed with his latest creation for himself. "Hey, Ros, see about some feathers back there, red ones. I'm getting this number together, baby. Ros, it's hot!" he said as he held up a satin jumpsuit that plunged to just below his dark nipples. "I got a singing date coming up. Check out those feathers, would you?"

"Solly, you want those earrings I told you about? The leftover, stray ones, partners to the ones I've lost?"

"Yeah, baby, slip 'em to me, I can dig 'em," he said. "Or I knows some people who can use 'em," he muttered, slowly stroking his thin chest and then his left earlobe. "Always looking for a bit of flash, baby!"

"I'm going to the back, call me if . . ."

"Yeah, yeah, yeah, now, don't you get naughty back there. Well, hello Dolly, hello Dolly, it's so nice to see you back where you belong. Red feathers, Ros. I can tell, Dolly. . . . You're looking swell, Dolly. . . . Far out and if this isn't the hottest thing that ever caressed this baby boy's sweet ever-loving ass!"

I kicked the foot stand back between the racks of costumes that hung in the darkness of the clothing warehouse. Henry VIII's costume clung to a dog's suit while Solange's plaid pinafore and apron soundlessly caressed Charlotte Corday's low-cut summer frock. Two metal racks, one eye-level, the other higher, followed the curved wall to the back of that mausoleum full of costumes waiting for a theatrical resurrection. A bodice here, a shirt there, shoes, and now a coat, and of course, tights, the black ones, with holes I had so patiently sewn, every other Wednesday from 8:30 to 11:30 A.M. It was my duty, my privilege, my honor to serve the great theater machine, an apprentice in the craft of camouflage.

As part of my weekly job, I was responsible for washing the actors' clothes and costumes. How far does art go, and when does pure unadulterated slavery begin? A cup of Amway soap couldn't really clean Jettie Brady's soiled underpants and spotted girdle.

I climbed down to the second floor the back way, meeting Rolla Larsen, the costume mistress, who was carrying a box of turquoise seam rippers in her hands, the kind that Solly Mathison liked to steal. I mumbled something while Rolla climbed the back stairs. I watched her large pleated ass disappear and snarled in her direction, still nervously trembling from my morning's breakfast of instant hot chocolate with water. Later I combed through the men's dressing room, extricating once-starched shirts and pairs of brown knickers, and a few dark socks. *The Crucible* was a play about fanaticism, but for the time being, its themes were dirty collars, sweat stains, and mismatched footwear.

Crossing the stairway, I went into the women's dressing room, where I sorted through lingerie, bringing into the light more of Jettie Brady's underclothes. Jettie Brady, the woman with the dyed and thinning blond hair, the long hook nose, the cold dispassionate blue eyes, and the yeast-stained panties, was in charge of all the apprentices. It was she I was accountable to.

How far does art go and when does slavery begin?

Jettie Brady was on her witch hunt in Salem present.

Standing in the elevator with Loudon's huge hands on my neck, I composed a letter in my mind. . . .

Dear Jettie:

I have been wanting to talk to you for a long time regarding the feudal conditions in the costume shop. Isn't there a way I could be moved to another work-study job in the theater? Rolla Larsen is unfair, unkind, dictatorial. I haven't been feeling well, Jettie, I wonder if . . .

I looked down at my hands. I have taken to reevaluating limbs every five years or so. My once skinny, bony hands with the long fingers now have suddenly become "artistic."

"My hands are blue. My hands are blue. Loudon, my hands are blue."

"Your hands are blue?" he said.

"God, my hands are blue! Loudon, I have to get out of this elevator."

"Come on, Rocío, just settle down. Two floors to go."

"Two floors to go!" Padded hysteria with two floors to go. "My hands have never turned blue before. Oh, they've been cold, Loudon, they're always cold, but this is different! From the wrist down, my hands are blue!"

"Rocío, now just get something to eat, okay?"

The elevator doors opened and Loudon quickly stepped in front of me and disappeared into the crush of faces at Roland Nevis's party for *The Crucible*. I knew about witch hunts. I faced the supreme Wicca, Lorna Preston, the speech teacher. She looked radiant, her long brown hair flowing over her shoulders, framing a cultured, prepared face. She was the witch, Abigail, regaling men over onion dip and crackers.

"Ma me mi mo mu," Lorna mouthed in speech class. "The lawyer's awfully awkward daughter ought to be taught to draw. EEEEEEEEEEEEEE—YOOOOOOO! Now repeat after me: MMMMEEEEE; PPPPPPPRRRRRRRRR- RREEEEE; WWWWWWWWEEEEEE; ME, ME, ME, PREE, PREE, PREE, WEE, WEE, WEE, and *remember:* Marilyn Monroe lips! Sexy, loose, and relaxed. That's why the English speak so well, have you seen their forward stretch? Watch my lips, watch me. . . ."

Every day she was the disheveled vituperous bitch; tonight she was Abigail before the fall, long-tressed, bright-faced, with puckered red lips, in a long, flowered peasant dress near the cheddar cheese balls.

Ron Lerner waved to me from across the room. He was so handsome, with his dark eyes and hair. He had the innocent, bewildered look of a maligned Lucifer prior to the moment of banishment. He was beautiful, vainglorious, expectant, hopeful, proud, and full of troubled hidden thoughts.

I waved to Ron and he motioned for me to cross to him. He took my hand, not noticing its inky hue. I wanted to forget the illness that crept up my arm, immobilizing goodness and filling me with dread, inquietude, and paranoia in the midst of celebration.

"Ron!"

"Come upstairs with me! Come on!"

"Ronald, how are you?"

"Let's go look at the room upstairs."

"Can you believe this house?"

"Nice, huh?"

"Have you eaten?"

"The Swedish meatballs."

"Hell, I don't know what I'd do, Ron, if I didn't eat well at these parties. Have you eaten mellorine? That's how bad it's gotten. I'm so tired of being poor."

"So let's go upstairs and look at the rooms, Rocío. Still looking for a place to live?"

"Do you know of anything?"

"How about the Robertson complex, where Loudon lives?"

"I don't know, I don't want to depend on Loudon. I need my own place. You still at the house on Emmett Hill?"

"Yeah. God, would you look at these rooms. Hey, Rocío, come in here with me."

I stepped inside the master bedroom. I could see myself in the three-way mirror with its veiled patterns of gray rivulets that ran across the mirror's expanse. The walls were lime green with white trim; the carpets were white and covered with shag fur. The toilet tank cover, the lid cover, and the base of the toilet were immaculate with snowy down. The soap dishes exuded lemon-scented freshness.

Ron stood behind me. I could see him in the mirror. I'm in love with you, I thought. Easily, carelessly, he traced the outline of my shoulders and back with his fingers. I wanted to say, "I love you, Ron. Why do you still live in the house on Emmett Hill?" But instead, I cleared my throat and stepped outside.

"I'll be right out," the dark angel said mysteriously.

Ron had locked the bathroom door. I sat in the hallway, waiting for him to exit. I stared at the beige wallpaper with its shadowed coronets. Loudon doesn't understand me. I have no home. I am homeless. Where can I move? Why won't Loudon let me stay with him? After all, we are friends. We're friends, aren't we? He's too busy, all his time taken up. Why do people get degrees? How many hearts broken, lovers abandoned? Loudon! Where's Ron? I'll just wait here. Sit down on this loveseat. Alone. Wait for Ron. My hands are blue. Why? I don't know, it's all too much. I don't have a place to live. Loudon doesn't want me. He's told me so.

Dear Jettie:
I just *have* to get out of the costume shop. Can't you find me another job? I'm afraid.

Ron! Where are you? What are you *doing* in there? Ron? Go downstairs to the party and eat something. Swedish meatballs. My hands aren't so blue. Ron, get out of the bathroom.

From where I sit I can see three doors. One. Two. Three. One of them is dark, one of them leads into another room, the last to the outside world. We are seven flights up. I'm going downstairs to talk to Loudon. Eat something. My hands aren't so blue. I don't know what to do. Ron, what are you doing in there? The house on Emmett Hill is filled with men. Lucifer is Lord. Ron is a misguided angel. He told me a story of growing up in hotels. Eugene O'Neill and Ron, playwrights born in hotel rooms, trying the rest of their lives to find homes, someone to love. Ron, I love you. Come out of the bathroom and talk to me. You could hold me if you want. That man with the blond beard, Leland, his bumpy chest in a black fishnet shirt, he lives on Emmett Hill. He and Raymond, one of the speech teachers, you live with them. Do they make love to you? Just come out of the bathroom and tell me. Ron, do they? We'll talk. That's all I need now. Someone to talk to. There are three doors. One. Two. And Three.

III

Kari Lee

This is my line. I've walked it so many dang times I'm getting dizzy. The part that really mixes me up is the part that comes at the beginning, that curved bend on the left that looks like a turkey's red hangy thing—the reason being that I gotta speed up coming out of a spin at that point, and loop around the top part, you could call it the head, and shoosh down, turning right, and then go into a bumpity hop hop hop hopping with a SUDDEN STOP.

My line reminds me of:

A turkey (I said this before).

A man's privates (golly, this is my notebook and I'm not sure I want Arlin or Miss E to see it—not to mention Mama! She thinks men's privates are dirty and ugly and who would want to see a man naked as a jaybird except someone sick). She says Michelangelo was sick and so are most artists. They got a fever can't be cured by anything, not even drugs. Miss E's an artist, but she's not sick. Miss M, well, she's a little funny, but not what you'd call SICK. More like WEIRD. Oh, I don't know, maybe only certain artists are sick, like Michelangelo and people from the past.

Miss E said to keep writing down what you think, but I don't know. When you're working with a line you're not supposed to let your thoughts stop even if they are stupid 'cause you never know when you might see a flash of light going off in your head. Inspiration it's called. "Perspiration is more like it," Arlin says in his snotty way. I keep getting confused and I start thinking about real people and real life and then I start wondering about this and that and about what they think about so and so and what so and so says and like Arlin says, "I'm just responding to stimuli."

My line reminds me of:

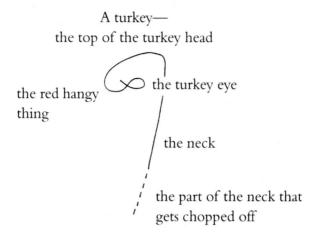

> A turkey—
> the top of the turkey head
>
> the red hangy
> thing   the turkey eye
>
> the neck
>
> the part of the neck that
> gets chopped off

Yuck. Now why'd I think of a headless turkey? Well, maybe it's okay 'cause Miss E says to stay with your line, walk it, skip it, hop it, dance it, and run it. I did and I got dang tired. Wouldn't you know it, Arlin Threadgill rode his line on a bike! Well, someone had to steady him at first, so it's no fair. The line was probably straight too. It's pretty incredible for a crippled kid like him to ride a line like that.

My line reminds me of:

Thanksgiving. If you turn it upside down, it looks like an amoeba, kind of, or a fetus that's whiplashing around, or a piece of wet wax that's drying up.

Now I'm getting tired of my line. But what can you do with it, once it's yours? Stick with it—until it has run itself through all it's gonna run through. All you can do is watch and listen and remember. This is my line. This is my line. It came to me. It came out of me. It's me, and now I want it to become Me-er than me.

Mama wouldn't understand my line. She has her own lines. Nobody would understand my line, except maybe Miss E, 'cause she understands things like how a person feels when she walks a line alone—twisting and turning and hopping yourself down to the end and stopping—and then beginning again. Now with sound:

MMMMMMMMMMMMMMMMMMMMMMMM
MMMMMMMMMMMMMMMMMMMMMMMM—tut tut tut,
ploom.

My line has a sound, a high-pitched cry—revving up and then dying out. Ploom. Ploom. Hard crash. The turkey neck falls to the ground.

My line reminds me of:

> All I can think are turkey thoughts, dang it!

IV

Rocío

The first time I saw Nita Wembley was the day of the garage sale at her White Elm Street apartments. I'd borrowed Loudon Reily's car, Cochise, to go apartment hunting. At that time I was living at the Robertson Estates with Loudon, in his bowling alley–shaped room, that under the influence reminded me of an alien spaceship. Come in, Captain Reily, this is Attendant Esquibel patching in. TALK TO ME. TALK TO ME. Beam me up to that place so that when we sleep we will travel together in dream.

"Have you ever read Mircea Eliade?"

"No, Loudon, who is she?"

"He! Ritual and Pathos, that sort of thing. Like Artaud."

"God, he was so handsome! What happened?"

"The artist demon in him . . . drugs, sex, bad teeth, the senses, and farther out . . . the greatest masturbatory experience . . . himself as . . ."

"He was so handsome. . . ."

"God, Rocío, are you there again? I was there ten minutes ago. Move on, would you? Jump! Your mind needs to jump! You get stuck!"

The garage sale consisted of a small rack of women's clothing, a dark crèpe de chine dress, a heavy navy blue pleated skirt, some children's clothing, pedal pushers, T-shirts, a winter coat with patches on the elbow, tablecloths, pot holders in bright colors, and a Persian lamb coat size 8 with the name Rose Marilyn hand sewn in the lining.

"Why, hello there. Now if that isn't a fit! It's got your name on it!"

"Rose Marilyn?"

"I'll have you know that this coat comes directly from the wife of a Baptist preacher. It's a fact! Now Quinnie Conklin, she sent this coat to me. It belonged to her sister-in-law that died of cancer."

"Rose Marilyn?"

"The same."

"Well, it's very pretty. Do you have a mirror?"

"Now, you just step in there to the ladies' room, through the hallway and see if it ain't *you* all over!"

"It *is* pretty!"

"And it fits so well, just like a glove. You need some gloves?"

"It's really pretty," I yelled from the empty bathroom. The apartment was bare except for a couch and a few wooden end tables.

"It's got your name on it, anybody with eyes can see that. Now looka here, it's a buy, you'd be a fool not to take it at ten dollars. Now there's a girl! It's just right for you, it's *you* all over. What you hemming for? Now take it, and that's that!"

Nita Wembley stood near the fireplace at the end of a large comfortable living room. She was a small woman, with a wrinkled, pink face. Her lips were incredibly thin, nonexistent almost and devoid of lipstick. She had no makeup on, and wore a thin gray-and-black Woolworth's scarf on her head over tiny blue rollers that pulled her wrinkles tightly toward her scalp. She wore a man's white shirt, buttoned incorrectly, causing the bottom of the shirt to hang down on one side like a ragged dog's ear. She was unkempt, in black stretch pants and once white, now gray sneakers with white crew socks.

"My name is Nita Wembley."

"I'm Rocío Esquibel. I'm a graduate student at the Drama Factory."

"You are? Why, maybe you know my little girl, Kari Lee Wembley?"

"Kari Lee Wembley? Is she your daughter? I have her in my Drama Appreciation III class."

"Why, you're *that* Miss Esquinel! I'd been waiting to meet you. By your name I thought you was Filipino. Why Kari Lee talks about you all the time. Miss Esquinel this and Miss Esquinel that. I declare."

"She's a nice girl."

"Yes, she is. I been sending her to Drama Appreciation class since she was in first. Mr. Wembley and I support the arts. Mr. Wembley is in the 100 Club. Yes, he is. We give regularly to that Factory, we do. We see all the plays, except when Mr. Wembley is working late, or if there is something, you know, not nice in the play."

"You're Kari Lee's mother? It's hard to believe."

"Oh, it is? Yes, I am Kari Lee's mama. I may not look it, but I am her mother. An old woman like me."

"Oh, no, that's not it, I mean, I'm just surprised to meet you!"

"Surprised? Expecting to see someone younger?"

"No, Kari Lee is a nice girl. She's very responsive and she's got a good imagination."

"That's a fact. She gets her imagination from me, not her daddy. Her daddy is another matter. Cloyd, that's Mr. Wembley. He's a doer, he don't have no time for imagination. Why, we've got the largest plumbing and heating business in Texas. Yes, we do! Our heaters are in all those skyscrapers in downtown Fort Worth, and we done the plumbing! Mr. Wembley and me, we built up our business outa hard work, Miss Esquinel."

"Esquibel."

"Miss Esquinel."

"Rocío."

"Miss Esquinel, we worked hard, slaving year in and year out. It ain't a fancified business that places you in front of society people with the Nevis-Springham name and ritzy parties. Me and Mr. Wembley are doers, we done it all and now there's Kari Lee to carry on. She come along when we didn't expect her and that is a fact! Maybe you're surprised, but Kari Lee is my natural-born daughter. She's not adopted. Now what business a woman my age doing having children? I'll tell you, Miss Esquinel. *None.* But the Lord manifested Himself. And that's that.

"It ain't easy, Miss Esquinel, me, a middle-aged woman, having worked hard all my life. Mr. Wembley works at the office and I run these here apartments. I am constantly cleaning up for the slobs that move in and out like vermin. One day I came in and found a mattress on this very floor and I said to myself, 'Nita Wembley, you get those hippies out of here this minute. I don't care what it takes. You get those dirty hippies out of here before they start having wild sex-filled parties and start smoking mary-wana and doing God knows what. Soon they'll be sleeping on the floor in one heap on that there mattress.' No, I'm too old to change, and too tired and too worn out and too much of a Christian woman to let no hippie atheists vandalize my apartment that I done worked so hard for all my life. Here I am, Lordy me, an older woman with a small child to take care of. You can imagine my surprise when Kari Lee came along. I'm fifty-one years old, Miss Esquinel."

"Why, you're so young!"

"No, Miss Esquinel, I'm old. An old woman, working out her last years. The Lord saw fit to send me a child and not only that, but to send me a Cross to bear in my later years."

"The apartment is vacant?"

"After all these years of hard work, me and Cloyd moved out to Oak Hill Estates. You know where that is? It's where the rich people live. And Miss Esquinel, we're rich! Little Kari Lee will inherit it all, because I tell you, I'm too tired and too worn out and too old and Cloyd ain't much better off. And what with my Cross, it's a heavy life, it is."

"Are you looking for a tenant?"

"Kari Lee came first and then my Cross, oh, the Lord knows why, I don't. Miss Esquinel, now, how do I look to you?"

"Fine, just fine, Mrs. Wembley."

"I don't look sick now?"

"Oh, no, you look just fine."

"Now, you forget the curlers and the clothes and look at me. Look at me. Real close. See anything wrong?"

"No, I . . . no . . ."

"Miss Esquinel, I don't have no breasts."

"You . . . ?"

"I am without the breasts the good Lord gave me. First Kari Lee and then, well, can you see, Miss Esquinel, after a life of working hard, God should send this tribulation from the Land of Cain."

"I'm . . ."

"Oh no, no, no, no. . . . Don't you be sorry. Sorry ain't enough. After all these years, sorry ain't enough. Now to look at me anyone would see a normal woman. Do you know what it is to have your female flesh cut away from you? Now I worked hard, I moved us from nowhere to the

Oak Hill Estates. We got a nice fancy house full of pretty things and Cloyd handles all the skyscrapers' accounts and we give to the Drama Factory. I believe in dreaming yourself something that you ain't. Now, Kari Lee, she's a good bright girl, she's gonna inherit all this. Well, sorry ain't enough. It just ain't enough. And that's that."

V

Kari Lee

Miss E and Miss M spread out a huge piece of butcher paper and then brought out a box full of cloth and sequins and felt and stuff like that. Me and Ginita Wall shared scissors and sat next to each other our knees touching, almost, and kinda smiling and laughing to ourselves.

"These are going to be our texture sheets," says Miss M.

"Texture sheets, are you kidding me?" shrieked Arlin. "What are they for?"

"On these sheets we'll design images from our minds. We'll take the cloth and rope and sequins and make a texture sheet for our characters."

"I don't like my character."

"It's all right, Arlin, we'll work on it today. That's the karate black belt, right?"

"I don't want to do anything dumb in class."

"Let's give it a try. Now everyone, you can do whatever you want with your sheets. Put down the textures that you think your character might like or dislike. You can write down your thoughts on your sheet and color with the crayons too. Just get your images down on paper."

"I ain't got no images," Arlin said.

"I don't *have* any images," I corrected. "Golly, Ginita, but I wonder what I'll do about my character. I don't know if I should do likes or dislikes. Dang, if it isn't a turkey. I never could think of anything else for my nature study, so I guess I'll just have to have turkey images. So here goes. Turkeys like warm, tidy turkey textures and soft earth and birdseed and . . . I hate turkeys!"

"Just put down what you feel, Kari Lee," said Miss E.

"I don't feel nothing, Miss E, except bored," said Arlin.

"Me neither, Miss E," I said. "Oh, I don't feel bored, I mean, I just don't feel nothing one way or another about this dang turkey."

Ginita was jumping around all over the room and getting this and that for her texture sheet and it looked so nice already, it was full of lace and flowers. She's lucky, she's got a human character. Animals are hard. And dumb!

"Just go over to the texture box and feel things, Kari Lee, you might get some texture ideas!"

So I went over and stuck my hand in and I felt something wet and sticky.

"Aaaaahhhhh."

"What is it?"

"Miss E, Arlin put his old spitty waddy bubble gum in the texture box. And I touched it! Yucko!"

"Har har har," laughed Arlin, that PILL. He musta petooied it with his lips. Anyway, what business did he have in the texture box, he don't got no hands, I wanted to say, but I didn't. Instead I just went back to my spot on the floor and drew a turkey like I always draw turkeys, by outlining my hand with its bumpy, ridgey fingers, and then I filled in the spaces between the fingers with a wavy, webby line. Then I worked on the turkey head, drawing a nose or beak, and added a sequin eye, and then I cut up some material in different colors, brown and red and blue, and filled in the turkey body. It wasn't too hard after all.

Ginita was working on her laces and pearls and I was with my turkey feathers and Arlin was over in the corner not texturing anything. All he was doing was practicing karate kicks like he was Bruce Lee with arms. He got tired after a while and sat down and looked kinda sad and, for the first time, I almost felt sorry for him. I must admit that by the end of the class, I was pooped too, but "Tom" was done, and I gave him to Miss E and she liked it well enough.

After class, Miss E and I sat together near the Coke machines talking while I was waiting for Mama to come and get me. Miss E said "Call me Rocío. Do you know I'm living at your mother's apartment on White Elm Street? It's real nice. I just got a cat, too, but don't tell your mama, because I'm not supposed to have cats."

"I won't," I said.

"I'll tell her about the cat soon. Her name is Oriene and she's a calico. Someday you'll see her. Your texture sheet is really something, Kari Lee. You're the only one in Drama Appreciation III class that's picked an animal to texture and character. That's something! Animals—they know, they feel, they respond, and they love."

"Yes," I said, "I know."

"They're smart. They're quiet and they listen and maybe even remember."

"They're like molecules," I said. "They have space and lines and texture."

"And they love you, quietlike and without reproach," said Miss E with a dreamy stare.

"For always," I said.

"Yes," said Miss E.

Gosh, I thought to myself, but Miss E's texture is so nice.

"Bye, now, Kari Lee. You take care and say hello to your mama. See you next week."

That's what Miss E said to me after class when we were sitting next to the Coke machine near the stairs going up to the theater lobby. No one was around but us two, eating melty Butterfingers that Miss E had in her purse. We washed the pieces down with cold Dr Peppers and talked about nothing, anything, and everything.

VI

Rocío

November the tenth. Walked back from the theater in darkness. I wish I had a car. The end of another day of slavery, albeit self-imposed. I stopped in the park near White Elm Street and watched the sky for traces. There were a few stars. They occasionally peeped through that vast sky like oiled beads.

I'm tired.

Class 8:30 to 11:30, lunch, and then work on Ionesco's *War Games.* In one scene a dying person reaches out. No one is there, but he imagines invisible hands holding him. He is consoled and peacefully leaves his tortured flesh. Next to him a woman cries out in terror: "Hold me, hold me, hold me! I'm afraid and it's dark! Hold me!" She is smothered with touches, caresses, her lover and family nearby. She imagines she is alone. She dies, crying out.

I found a dead bird next to the park bench. The darkened grass was wet; my feet sank into the earth. I wrapped the dead bird in white notebook paper. I spun around, hearing someone. Someone called out—a stranger. "Hey, hey you!" I was afraid, walked briskly toward home.

Bury it, Rocío. Bury it.

The overhead stars were obscured by clouds. They were bright sinkholes pulling light. I imagined that a passing plane was a spaceship with its flashing lights. I wanted to be taken. Freed.

Instead, I quickly walked the remaining blocks to the Wembley house. Joe's light was on. He was studying or eating supper by himself. I am in love with Joe, his blond strength, his violet eyes, his sureness, and his sorrow. Joe was married to someone in the theater, but he found her in bed with someone else.

May you never live to see the day.

"He doesn't talk about it," Loudon said to me.

Joe was Loudon's best friend, Joseph Pappas, the actor with the thinning hair, the long legs, Joseph eating alone, his bright light in the window. My next-door neighbor. Joe said to me the other day, "Wembley's crazy, Rocío, remember that!"

"Joe," I said, "but I need a place to live! At least you're a man and she doesn't bother you. Does she go on about her breasts to you? I can't take it anymore!"

"She's gone on enough, but her breasts, God forbid, no!"

"Only a woman," I said, "would willingly inflict herself on another woman that way."

"She's crazy, all right," he said, whistling in disbelief.

"It's Kari Lee I feel sorry for."

"Oh yeah, her."

Joe moved toward the door of his small apartment. I wanted to peer inside, be invited over, but it was unthinkable. I was Loudon's girl, and after what Joe had been through, with his ex-wife, the scenes, the infidelity, the confrontation, all of which I had vividly imagined, a cup of tea was impossible.

"See you, Joe."

"Just remember what I told you, Rocío. The woman's mad! Just remember that and pay your rent on time!"

The dead bird lay on the back porch. I fumbled for the key. I searched through my purse, impatient and talking to myself. No key. I'd have to break in. But how? The last time I'd used a dinner knife to pry open a window just above my head. I'd found it on the ground near the house. The knife was cold and it had slipped from my grasp and cut me in the upper lip. I bled profusely, cursing Loudon Reily all the way back to the Robertson Estates.

"Damn you, damn you, Loudon! Loudon, Loudon, why won't you help me?"

The knife was nearby and the window had been fixed. Damn Loudon for fixing the damn window. I broke the glass again, shards flew about me, falling to the wooden perch with a tinkle.

Bury it, Rocío. Bury it all. The dead bird was waiting. Now that was the problem. One of the problems. Nita Wembley let me move into her apartment even though she knew

I was poor. I received a two-hundred-dollar-a-month stipend and the rent was two hundred dollars a month.

"Miss Esquinel, the first month you can pay one hundred. I'll help you out. How about that?"

"Why, Mrs. Wembley, that's so nice of you! Yes, it would really help me out. But after that I'm not sure I can . . ."

"After that is a time from now."

"Yes."

"I'm doing this 'cause of Kari Lee and her drama education, mind you."

It was now the tenth of November and my second month's rent was past due. I had no money until the end of the month. I would have to call Mrs. Wembley, but what would I say? Could Loudon, no, not Loudon, never Loudon. As far as my family was concerned, they'd already sent me a hundred dollars and I was too ashamed to ask for more.

"And because I'm a Christian woman, Miss Esquinel."

As I opened the door, my schizophrenic pregnant cat escaped. Damn the cat! She'd come back to eat. They all come back screeching help me help me in the glowing darkness.

I turned on the light. It was late, about 10 p.m. Loudon was at home, working on his thesis. No doubt he was stoned on grass and music and himself. I dug a hole in the cold ground close to the house and buried the dead bird, covering it with earth. Then I took the rusty, silver-plated knife inside. In the refrigerator there was cat food and cold leftover macaroni.

I could hear Joe next door, practicing speech exercises. MA ME MI MO MU. He was Y-buzzing his way to fulfillment.

Having buried the dead bird, having washed my blue hands, having attempted to eat dinner, I lay down.

Dear Jettie:
I'm not feeling well. That's the reason I didn't attend class all last week. It's hard to explain. I can't eat. I choke on my food. My hands keep turning blue. Recently, I've started falling down stairs. I have no strength in my legs. I thought I broke my ankle the other day on the goat path behind the theater. But now I'm feeling better. I'm tired. God, I'm just so tired.

Oriene was meowing outside. When I let her in she followed me to bed, both of us shivering. She was very pregnant and huddled by my side, then got on my stomach and started moaning. She was oozing a brown bile; her juice was all over my blanket. Frightened and whimpering, she looked at me. She didn't know what was happening.

Oriene was scared, already birthing in my lap. I picked her up and said softly, "You must."

I placed her in the large closet in the hallway. Inside I had already arranged a bed for her. It was a straw mat covered by a sheet. She went to it, uncomprehending still.

Oriene! Oriene! If only I could . . . which reminded me of Ionesco's play. I thought of the dying man and woman. I ran my fingers over my forehead and face. Tired skin. Tired. Tired.

YYYYYYYYYYYYYYYYYYYYYYYYYYYYYYYYY-
YYYYYYYYYYYYYYYYYYYYY—OOOOOOOOO-
OOOOOOOOOOOOOOOOOOOOOOOOOOOOO-
OOOOOOOOOOOOO!

Joe's voice shrieked through the walls. YYYYOOOO! I heard the Irish brogue that signified clarity. After working through a multitude of speech exercises, one always ended with this last one, the one that completely opened up your voice.

My boyfriend Loudon was working on his thesis. His play was about communicating without words.

You thought you were brighter and smarter and better than me, Loudon. You were the captain. You left me behind. You were always ahead of me, and let me know it.

I turned off the overhead light, my head buzzing in silence. I got up and wrote in my journal:

> The blindness of white on white
> the moss of tree on tree
> plant over plant
> the flowing liquid green—my silence—
> was crying to throw itself down

and then I wrote on another page:

> Sorrowed death trance of fear
> living
>
> Remember the funny lady
> with the little blue hat

Texas in April
was one time

Climbing up flights
going down to Holy Places
around the block

Impaled, we
were.

VII

The Wembleys

"Open the door. It's Miss Esquinel a ringing. I saw her from the window. She's a Spanish girl. You know what pretty hair their people have."

"Esquibel, Mama! She's so pretty and so nice and all the kids like her, they do, Mama!"

"Kari Lee Wembley, you open that door! Miss Esquinel's waiting. She may be nice, but she's two weeks late with her rent."

"Mama, I'll get it!"

"Well, go on then, get the door!"

"Miss E!"

"Kari Lee!"

"Hi."

"Ask Miss Esquinel in, Kari Lee."

"I really can't stay long, Mrs. Wembley. I just came by to bring the rent. I'm sorry I'm late but . . ."

"It's all right now, you just step in here and sit down, Miss Esquinel."

"Oh, Mrs. Wembley, your house is lovely!"

"It's a pretty house, there's no denying. Now get out of the way Kari Lee and let Miss Esquinel look around."

"It's very nice, Mrs. Wembley."

"Yes it is. I worked hard for all of this, I'll have you know, all my life I worked to move into this neighborhood, and no one's gonna take me from it, exceptin' the Good Lord when he calls me home."

"You want to sit down, Miss E?"

"The name's Esquinel, Kari Lee, you call her *Miss* Esquinel."

"I told all the kids to call me Rocío, or Miss E, Mrs. Wembley."

"Now, do you think that's right, Miss Esquinel, all that familiarity? Now come over here to this couch, won't you?"

"I wanted to come by and tell you how sorry I am for not bringing the rent sooner. I got busy at school. Mrs. Wembley, I *really* am grateful to you for letting me live in the apartment. It's lovely, so nice and clean."

"How's Oriene, Miss E?"

"Oriene, who's that, Kari Lee? I *did* rent that apartment to a bachelor girl, Miss Esquinel!"

"It's her cat, Mama!"

"All my places are clean, Miss Esquinel. I clean 'em myself. Look at my hands. They're ugly. They are. I've worked them hard. I don't hire no one to clean my places. I clean them myself, no fancy maids for me, and I clean my own house, and it's big. I done it all by myself in the past. I'll do it by myself in the future. So, you watch that animal, young woman."

"It's a beautiful house."

"Yes it is. Kari Lee, you got any homework?"

"Mama, hardly none."

"Now, run along and play. I want to talk to Miss Esquinel alone."

"Mama, I got hardly nothing to do and it's almost suppertime."

"Now, Kari Lee Wembley, don't you be crossing me, go and do your homework."

"Aaaaaaaaaaright, Mama. Bye, Miss E, see you next week, okay? I've been working on my nature study gobs. My turkey, remember?"

"That's wonderful, Kari Lee! See you later."

"Bye."

"She's such a nice girl."

"Yes, she is. But I don't know, Miss Esquinel, I have to tell you, it's a difficulty having a youngster when a person's already tired out. She ain't no trouble to me and Cloyd, that's Mr. Wembley, but all the same, it's not easy and then there's my Cross. I never suspected the Lord smite me for my sins. It's the truth. I done all I could my life, working hard building up the plumbing business with Cloyd and to have the Lord . . ."

"I brought the rent."

"Just leave it there on that coffee table, Miss Esquinel. We got everything we need or want, Miss Esquinel. Kari Lee ain't lacking for a thing. Oooohh!"

Nita Wembley sighed, then placed both hands on her vacant breasts.

"It's a Cross same as I breathe."

Nita started to cry the dried, long-withheld tears of someone who hadn't cried in years.

"I never cry much, must be the tiredness."

"Mrs. Wembley, you'll be okay. You're alive and you have a family that loves you."

"You a churchgoer?"

"I am. . . ."

"Catholic, like all your people?"

"You're so lucky, Mrs. Wembley. You have so many things to be grateful for, your work, this house, Kari Lee. . . ."

"Ohhhh Lord!" Nita Wembley called out. She fingered the buttons on her blouse. She was dressed in a man's blue work shirt with a pair of soft-looking, much washed jeans and the same pair of grimy tennis shoes. Her hair was in tight curls, like a little girl's. She wore no makeup. Her dry, transparent skin resembled the stretched leather of thirsty, dying animals.

Mrs. Wembley unbuttoned her work shirt, pulled up her faded white T-shirt, and showed me her ravaged breasts.

I sat in the brilliant sunlight of early evening, facing Nita Wembley's pinched, scarred, inverted chest.

She looked at me closely, then looked at her breasts with contempt.

"You're a child," she said. "The Lord spare you this."

Slowly, she lowered her T-shirt, buttoned her work shirt, tucked it in with calloused fingers, and sat facing me. A cloud rambled past the room and it grew dark. The tables and lamps cast long shadows on the walls. The ashtrays, ornaments, and cut-glass figurines exuded a crystalline composure. The room was silent, large. I fingered the rent envelope, cleared my throat.

Nita Wembley faced me.

"Me, working hard all my life . . . for this . . ." she said, with disgust and horror.

Cochise was waiting outside. Loudon was writing his play on the other side of town.

Just then a man entered the room. Mrs. Wembley turned on a huge, three-way lamp that was positioned near her. Our island was furnished now with light.

"Cloyd Wembley, Kari Lee's daddy."

Mr. Wembley nodded to me courteously, saying nothing.

"It's nice to meet you, Mr. Wembley."

"Now, Cloyd, you go on back and clean up and I'll get you supper."

I stared into Cloyd Wembley's face. He was a lean, weathered man with a bulbous nose covered by enormous blackheads of some fifty years' standing. They were dark and large, blocking innumerable pores. They were plugs the likes of which are rarely seen.

Cloyd Wembley wore dark gray work clothes, a green striped work cap, and work boots. His large, hairy arms were splattered with tiny flecks of mud and dried cement. When he took off his hat, I saw the marks of rimmed sunburn and sweat that attested to manual labor. His hair was plastered down and full of dandruff. He smelled like an overheated goat: acrid, meaty.

The handshake was quick, firm, and left me with moist fingertips.

"Now, Cloyd, you go on. Clean up."

Cloyd Wembley bowed and walked to the back of the house. He had a quiet dignity that had survived his marriage of thirty-six years to the shrill, long-suffering Nita Wembley, née Humphries.

"That's Mr. Wembley. Man's a mess now."

"Mrs. Wembley, I better go."

"I know."

"Thank you."

"I'll show you to the door, Miss Esquinel. Time for Mr. Wembley's supper."

"Your house is lovely. Really. Oh, and by the way, I'll be leaving for Christmas vacation in a few weeks. Joe is going to look after things."

"Yes, it is a nice house," she said, looking around appreciatively.

"I'll be more prompt with my rent payment next month."

"Now you watch that cat, Miss Esquinel. Cats got a foul body smell, you let them run wild and scratch the chairs and furniture, not to mention them doing the necessities on the floor and rugs."

"She's a well-behaved cat, trained."

"No wild animal is ever completely trained. People tell me they gonna keep their pet on a leash and I find doggie-do in the corners when I clean up. Had to fumigate the rugs and call in someone to help me, it was so bad one time. You gonna take the cat home with you?"

"No, I've asked Joe to feed her."

"Joe Pappas gonna feed her?"

"Good-bye, Mrs. Wembley. If I don't see you, Merry Christmas!"

"You watch that animal! No tenant of mine is gonna run wild with their animals. It's the same as living in filth!"

"Thank you again!"

I raced down the steps, my knees secure, no problem of falling down, back to the comforting metallic barriers of Cochise. Nita Wembley waved to me and went back into her

Oak Hill mansion. I sat in Cochise, breathing hard, all the windows raised. I was trembling, sick, anxious with the overwhelming weight of Nita Wembley's vile, unstable confessions of guilt and pain. Twelve shopping days till Christmas.

VIII

Rocío

"Want some?"

"No, Loudon. I'm too nervous to smoke."

"Forget it, R, let it go."

"I can't. I feel so empty, so helpless."

"Listen to some music."

"Have you eaten, Loudon?"

"No, you want some food?"

"I'm hungry, but I'm too tired to swallow."

"What *is* your problem?"

"I'm just tired."

"You're always tired."

"Yes, I am."

"Damn it, stop crying."

"Loudon, I . . ."

"You can stay here tonight. You want to stay here tonight, Rocío?"

"I don't know, I'm just so tired."

"Why don't you do something about it, see a doctor?"

"I don't have any money. If I could just stop, rest, get away from things. I'm so tired and empty and alone. I'm so depressed."

"Go to bed, then."

"Just hold me, would you?"

"Rocío, you okay?"

"Yeah, I'm okay. I'll go to bed. Sleep."

"You aren't hungry?"

"Got something soft? Something I can eat and not think about swallowing?"

"Milk?"

"Yeah, I'll get it. You want some?"

"Sit here, Rocío, you gotta get yourself together. Jettie was telling me that you've been missing class, that you're never in school. *What* have you been doing?"

"Sleeping. I'm just so tired. I can't get up."

"Are you sick?"

"I don't feel good. Most of all, I'm just tired and empty. Like nothing was inside."

"Rocío, honey, go to bed. Okay?"

"I haven't fed Oriene and the kittens."

"She can wait until tomorrow."

"Loudon, I'm sorry for not feeling . . ."

"Yeah, it's okay. Just go to bed! I have some work to do, my advisor is waiting for a new draft on the introductory chapter."

"I can go home."

"No, you can stay tonight."

"I'm sorry that you had to move your papers."

"It's okay."

"Really, I can go. Would you give me a ride? I'm so tired."

"Rocío!"

"All right, I'll stay. Good night, Loudon. I love you."

"Go to bed!"

Sometimes when I lie down in the spaceship I am frightened. I feel voices on either side, converging in the middle of my head, splitting me apart. Loudon is the first man I have ever lived with; if only he would let me live with him. He is the first man I have slept with, if only he would sleep with me now, my body fully against him, the two halves of a whole. If only he weren't so heavy. When he lays his arm on top of me, I say, "Loudon, Loudon, your arm, move it. It's too heavy." He complains bitterly and mutters, *"What's wrong with you?"*

"I'm tired, that's all."

If I could just rest.

When I fall asleep I hear voices and they talk to me and I see faces. Faces of people I know, except they aren't the real faces, but the faces of impostors, all of them. And yet, I want to believe. I want to believe!

"You're always so tired," Loudon says.

"I'm so tired of being tired!"

I want to believe. I want to believe. I want to believe!

When I woke up the next morning, Loudon was peering out the window, secretively, furtively.

"Goddammit! Hasn't got any decency! Parading out there for everyone to see!"

"What is it, Loudon? What's going on?"

"Out there in her damn underwear for all the world to see!"

"What?"

"Standing out there throwing her garbage."

"Who is it?"

I stared out the window across to the vacant parking lot next door. A woman was out there in her white bra and panties throwing garbage. I couldn't make out who she was. I was still unsteady on my feet and bleary-eyed.

"It's Charene," Loudon said contemptuously, while at the same time craning his neck to see her as best he could.

"That's Charene? In her underwear? Throwing out the garbage?"

"She does it all the time."

"Loudon, I'm going to school. I wondered if you could stop in and check on Oriene and the kittens. You know, feed them."

"I can't do that, R, my thesis."

"Oh," I said limply, going to my clothes.

"You okay today?"

"I'm hungry, you hungry?"

"Eat some eggs."

"Loudon, what do you think is wrong with me?"

Loudon was at the window, staring out, the curtain folded in front of his face, allowing him to see and not be seen.

"Dammit!" he said emotionally. "Damn whore. Here she comes again. More garbage!"

IX

Nita

"That filthy animal smell of cat! I couldn't hardly make it in the door and then I see cat food all over the kitchen floor and then I see the curtains all torn up and hanging there, and on checking the other rooms, I see four cats in there with the big one, the mama, them all stretched out comfortable as can be.

"She lied to me, the filth and the smell and the cats like all those hippie people trashing out a decent Christian place and not paying the rent on time this month or the last and me finally having to go down there and demand my honest hard-earned money and here I says, me, trusting you and you lying to me and messing the place up and me trying to help you, and giving you a chance. I knowed you didn't have the full rent that first month, so I tried to help you, give you a break on account of you being Kari Lee's Drama Appreciation III teacher and me thinking you was different than the rest like the time you came over and talked and I shared with you certain things.

"But you're not so different after all. Well, I can tell you this, young woman, I'll call Mr. Trevor at the school and tell him, bet you I will. I'll tell him, being the head of the Drama Factory, about the rent and the apartment and the cats and how you lied to me and that you ain't fit to be in school studying dramatics much less teaching children. You'll be sorry you ever came to know Nita Wembley.

"I worked hard all my blessed life, I can't say this enough. It ain't just all the troubles and the sorrows and the coming of Kari Lee and then my Cross and then those hippies with the little baby and now you—a supposed LADY—but underneath it all, you're the same, hippies living in filth. It's something else. And about that you know nothing. Nothing!

"I'll call Mr. Trevor and tell him all about you and how you lied to me, and me, unsuspecting, showing you the cup of human kindness, more than human kindness. You'll be sorry you ever ran into Nita Humphries Wembley. Me, a Christian God-fearing woman, someone who's worked hard all her life and knows what it is to struggle every single day.

"Well, I tell you now. Sorry ain't enough!"

X
Rocío

Charene called out to me as I walked up the stairs to the costume shop. It was a Wednesday.

"Rocío!"

"Hello, Charene."

"What's this I hear about you not paying your rent and trashing out Mrs. Wembley's apartment during Christmas break?"

"What?"

"I heard you let your cats run loose in the house and they managed to tear up all the furniture and shred the curtains."

"What? Who told you that?"

"Now look here, Rocío, I'm telling you now that you better get your act together or you're going to be out on your ass. You'll have to start really thinking about what you're doing. Do you know that Mrs. Wembley's one of the theater's patrons? She's a Golden Angel and Mr. Wembley is in the 100 Club and *that* means that she can do and say anything she damn well pleases around here and that we here at the theater listen to her. Do you understand that, Rocío? That means that you better damn well get your priorities and problems and shit together and stop screwing around with members of the 100 Club. Do you understand me?"

"Now, Charene, just wait a minute! I don't see that this is any of your business."

"It *is* my business as house manager of this theater and don't you forget *who* you're talking to."

"I don't think you know very much about what's going on."

"I know about you, and how you've been skipping class and carrying on. Jettie and Mr. Trevor told me. I talked to Jettie and she says if you don't start going to class soon, they're gonna kick you out on your ass, so you better watch it! You're not the person to be messing with me or Mr. Trevor or Nita Wembley!"

"Who told you about this?"

"Get your shit together and stop acting like you're so helpless. Do you hear me?"

"Now just a minute, Charene. Let me explain!"

"Dammit, do you hear me? Stop messing around!"

"How did you hear all this?"

"Mrs. Wembley called Mr. Trevor."

"She did?"

"Do you understand me? Do you? NITA WEMBLEY IS A GODDAMN GOLDEN ANGEL AND IN THE 100 CLUB AND NO ONE, NOT EVEN YOU, BITCH, MESSES WITH HER! GOT IT?"

Charene Easterman gave me a disgusted look and stomped up the stairs into the lobby, where she was to lead a tour of French diplomats around the theater. She was a native speaker. Oooohhh mais oui! Charene looked radiant. She was a physically beautiful woman, well-endowed, with golden blond hair. With her back to me, she smiled to the crowd.

I climbed the stairs to the costume shop, sidestepping Rolla Larsen, who was arguing with Solly Mathison, accusing him of stealing fabric from the costume shop for his own personal use. I entered the darkness of the clothing room, found my way past the clothing racks, humid with lost words, indecisive acts, and sat in the small room in the back, on a metal stool, folding tights. I sat in silence, too tired to cry.

XI

Loudon

Rocío said, "Take me to Albertson's so I can get things for tonight."

Joe was coming over for tacos, Rocío's specialty. She wanted it to be a good meal. When we got to Albertson's she was afraid to go inside, she said the lights were too bright and she didn't know if she could make it in. And once she got inside, she said, "Loudon, I have to get out. I can't breathe. I need some fresh air."

So, she went outside and stood by the automatic door, looking pale and nervous.

"What's wrong with you?" I said. "Go and see a doctor!"

And then she started to cry.

"Oh, just give me a list of things you need and I'll get them."

"No, I've got to do it," she said. "Don't leave me, Loudon, I'm sick."

She went to lie down after we got home and she was crying and then she got up and said, "Hold me."

"Maybe you should lie down," I said. She was still crying.

"No, no, no, no, if I lie down, I'll die. I don't want to die. I have to make tacos."

She kept saying something about the play she was working on and about dying alone, even if someone was there, and that scared me. I knew she wasn't all right then, but hell, she wouldn't eat anything and she was skinny as can be, and nervous. Very nervous. There she was, standing over the stove mashing the taco meat and chopping onions and running around and every once in a while she would lie down, but then she'd spring up and start mashing again. She seemed to be okay after a while. Joe came over with his new girlfriend and the food was good and I stayed there overnight to see if R was going to be okay.

The next day she decided to move out of her White Elm Street apartment, and said, "I really shouldn't have a cat. Poor thing, it's not fair, she's as crazy as me."

So that next weekend we drove Cochise into the country to her cousin's and R found homes for all the kittens, and then she moved to an apartment on Bowser Street for seventy-five dollars a month. Oh, it's lousy and dark. She says the bathroom is full of spiders. I don't like to go over there unless I have to, but I haven't told her that. She says she mostly just sleeps there and it doesn't matter. She walks to school from there.

Most of the time she stays with me nights and goes home to change. Her mother called over to my place the other night and I heard R explain to her all that had happened. She told me later that her mother told her (being on a hot line for sick people) that she had had a nervous breakdown, almost.

"Aw, come on," I said, "are you kidding me? No way, man!"

"It's the little things that go wrong and they just keep adding up," she said. "Until one day something really little happens. It might not really be that little, but then it doesn't matter anymore. And then you just disappear. You just disappear."

"Hell, Rocío, you're okay, what are you talking about?"

And she turned to me and said, "If it weren't for the tacos, Loudon, I don't know *how* I could have made it."

XII

Kari Lee

Today in class Miss E says we're going to write. Maybe it will help our nature study.

"What we're going to write is something called 'The History of a Friendship.' "

Miss E talks about a friend—a real close friend—Ramona somebody who got mad at her. I guess that's what happened. Miss E says she never really knew for sure what happened, but one day Ramona wouldn't talk to her and ever since then, she's still barely even said hello.

"I've tried to be nice and still, she doesn't talk to me," Miss E said. "I called her up several times, but someone else answered. They said she was at her tennis class. And when I left a message for her to call back, she never answered."

This made Miss E sad and her voice was kinda quavery and for once Arlin Threadgill was quiet and listening.

"And so what happened?" asked Arlin.

"Nothing, except I guess that I'll try again someday. Have any of you ever felt that way?" she asked.

Miss E looked so pale and sick. She was out of class for a couple of weeks and she just came back today. Arlin said she was *real* sick.

"So, how'd you find out, creep?"

"My mother told me, double triple creep."

So we talked about it in the hallway and for the second time ever I looked at Arlin Threadgill and he wasn't a crippled boy, he was normal-like. And I felt sad, I could still hear my mama saying mean things about Miss E, things like: "Kari Lee, you stay away from that hippie. You stay away. She's done your mama harm. I tried to be her friend, Kari Lee, but she lied to me. She's filth, she's filth!"

"Oh, Mama!" I cried in my room later. "But she's my *friend*. She's my *friend*!"

"Ain't you mine, Kari Lee Wembley?"

"Yes," I said, "oh yes, but Mama, you don't understand. She and I are molecules."

And then Miss E's voice said, "Has it ever happened to you that you think you have a friend and you don't?"

"Yes," I said, and so did Ginita Wall.

"Well, let's write about that. Tell me about a friendship of yours, maybe it was happy and maybe it was sad. Maybe it's like me and Ramona, where something went wrong, except one person just can't figure it out."

"Oh, all right," said Arlin.

"Does anyone need any help?" asked Miss E.

"Not me," said Arlin, "have I got a story. . . ."

"I'm sure it is, Arlin! That's good, that's very good. . . ."

Ginita Wall raised her hand and asked politely, "Miss E, can we use space and line and texture and anything we want with our stories?"

"Of course, Ginita," Miss E said, sitting down. "Now, while you're writing *your* stories, I'll write *mine.* Everyone got a pencil?"

"I've got a pen," said Arlin.

Everybody found their very special alone place. Miss E looked at me like she liked me so much, but I turned away 'cause I remembered what Mama told me about Miss Esquibel and I felt sick and sad.

I don't know. I can never think when it comes down to the thinking part. I guess I'll just have to jump in and see what happens. I felt hot and something else I couldn't describe. I decided to start my thinking again. Miss Esquibel was all hunched up, chewing on a pencil, and thinking real hard. I don't know. She looked so busy writing. Once she looked up in my direction, kinda wild-eyed, not really seeing me, but looking out past me, as if she was concentrating on something real hard. You know that wild-eyed look of someone concentrating.

So I looked at my paper and with a kinda shaky hand I wrote:

HISTORY OF A FRIENDSHIP
by Kari Lee Wembley
Theatre Appreciation III Class
KARI LEE WEMBLEY = 6
ROCIO ESQUIBEL = 6

And I thought to myself, "If space is a solid, then what is the shape of darkness?"

COMPADRE

I

"Llévale un vaso de agua."

"What?"

"Take him a glass of water."

"What?"

"Take Regino a glass of water, Rocío!"

"Where is he?"

"Outside in the backyard. It's hot!"

"We don't have ice. The freezer is jam-packed; a tray wouldn't fit."

"Then take something out!"

"What can I take out? The freezer is full of green chile. What do you want me to do with it? Let it rot? Oh, everything is a mess. There's no room in the freezer for ice, all there is is chile and more chile and some old, what is this, meat? Is this meat in here? It looks old."

"Let me see, it's ham."

"Ham? This is ham? Where'd we get it, Mother?"

"Regino's compadre works at the packing plant, he got us the ham."

"There's no room for ice!"

"Put some good water in the refrigerator."

"I did and somebody drank from the bottle and left the cap unscrewed and then scooped watermelon from the middle, dripping seeds and juice all over the icebox and into the water that was in the bottle."

"It's not an icebox," Mercy yelled from the living room, where she sat reading *Ozma from Oz*. "*When* are you going to stop saying icebox? It's 1962, Rocío!"

"I can say icebox if I want to, Mercy; who's talking to you anyway? Just shut up in there."

"Don't say shut up to your sister, Rocío. In my house you will not say shut up. . . . It's vulgar. You will *not* say shut up to your sister, or to anyone else! Do you understand me?"

"Mother! It's just a way of expressing . . . Oh, what's the use? *Everything* is wrong! Everything! I hate this house, it's so junky and messy and crammed full of crap. . . . Look at this freezer, you can't even put in a tray of ice. We *never* have ice; when people come over, we have to give them lukewarm water from the tap. . . ."

"It's good water, not as good as Texas water, but good."

"That's not what I'm talking about. *This* is what I'm talking about, this mess, this house, all of it jam-packed with crap. I hate this house, you can never find anything, there's so many newspapers and magazines and things! Let me clean it up, throw things away. You can't even get through the back room anymore. The last time I went up to the attic I thought I'd suffocate. It's crowded and dusty and dark and . . . I wish this house would burn down! I just wish it would burn down so we could start all over again! We'd get rid of . . ."

"Rocío! Don't say that. You don't mean that! It's our house and it will not burn down, I tell you, it won't burn down, and don't you curse it! I love this house, your daddy built this house, you were born here, and we've lived here ever since. This house is fifteen years old and it's full of *us*, our things. . . . You will not curse my house!"

"I'm not cursing! Have I cursed? You don't know what cursing is. All I'm talking about is . . . Will you listen to me?"

"I don't want to talk. . . ."

"Then listen to me, Mother, will you just *listen*? I'm talking about this junk. It's a fire hazard. We could go up in flames, but no, we have to keep the old newspapers and the *Reader's Digest*s and the *Life* magazines . . . We have to! *That's* what I'm talking about! That's what I'm talking about. *This!*"

"Someday they'll be valuable, Rocío! I like to look at them. Sometimes I just go to the back room and look at old magazines. I found a picture of Lindbergh and his family!"

"Mother! Let me clean it up. I'll save the important things. It's too crowded. There's no space. I can't find anything anymore."

"No. And that's final."

"Oh God. Well then, has anyone seen my book? I lost it again."

"What book?" Mercy yelled from the living room.

"Don't yell," Mother said softly. "And don't curse. You will not curse in this house!"

"God, my book, the one I've been reading for weeks. *Gone with the Wind*."

"You're still reading that?" Mercy asked, coming into the kitchen and sitting on the blue linoleum counter. She took a banana from the metal lazy Susan. "I read it already."

"You did, Mercy?" Mother said incredulously. "When?"

"Oh, before."

"Where's my book?"

"Why don't you clean house today?" Mother answered.

"Mother! I can clean house any day. It's summer! Who wants to clean house?"

"If you're so interested in throwing things out, clean the house. Maybe you can find something to throw out."

"Someone has taken my book again! And it was the same person that dripped watermelon seeds in the icebox."

"Refrigerator!"

"Shut up!"

"God, it was disgusting!"

"It wasn't me," said Mercy.

"Where's my book?" I demanded.

"I don't know."

"Are you almost done?" said Mercy, munching the banana.

"No, I'm not almost done. Who asked you to come in here and join the conversation? You stole my book, Mercy!"

"It's in Mother's closet. I saw it there, Rocío!"

"Mother! Did you take my book?"

"No. Yes. Yes, I took your book. Ever since you started reading that book you've done nothing around the house. Nothing! Look at mi compadre out there, sweating! Why don't you clean house, work in the yard, *do* something!"

"It's summer!"

"And not only that, do you think you should be reading that book?"

"*Gone with the Wind?* What do you mean? Mercy read it already."

"Shouldn't you be reading something else, Rocío?"

"*Goona from Oz,* maybe?"

"*Ozma,* and it's good."

"Oh, go away!"

"Don't you tell anyone to go away, Rocío. This is *my* house and you will not tell anyone to go away, *ever!*"

"I'm tired."

"Yes, you should be tired. You got up at noon!"

"It's summer!"

"It's not normal to be sleeping all day. If you were a diabetic, I could understand. If you were old, I could understand. If you were your father, I could understand."

"Please, Mother!"

"Okay, okay!"

"Can't we just throw away the newspapers and magazines? Is that too much to ask?"

"Who is that outside?" Mercy said, staring out the kitchen window, leaning over the cactus and pricking herself. "Ouch!"

"Compadre Regino."

"Oh, what's he doing?"

"Pulling weeds."

"Ugh."

"God! He's got a job there. No way in the world I . . ."

"I will not have you . . ."

"Mother, please!"

". . . say God like that in *my* house!"

"He's pulling the weeds, all right. It looks a lot better!"

"It does," said Mother, startled from her fury. "Yes, it does! Ooooh, compadre, ¿cómo le va? ¡Ooooooohhh!" Mother said, leaning toward the open window and screeching in an unnaturally expansive voice. "¿No quiere un vaso de agua o una limonada?"

"What's he saying, Rocío?"

"I can't hear from here."

"So go look, dummy!"

"Don't you call your sister a dummy, María Merced!"

"He's nodding yes. To what?"

"¿Limonada?"

"¿Agua?"

"¿Agua? ¡Agua! ¡Allí voy!"

Mother waved to compadre Regino as he stood in the hot July afternoon sun chopping weeds in our weather-beaten backyard. The dark red and black fence was down, having fallen over in an illegal garbage fire that spread to the rest of the yard. It hung like so many charred and broken matchsticks. Beside the fence stood a dried row of fruit trees: a lone cherry whose only fruit that year had been devoured selfishly by Mercy, and two listless peach trees, the larger distinguished by its singularly splayed, desiccated branches, the other shorter, no less dry.

Regino Suárez, the neighborhood handyman, had dug trenches leading from one tree to another, to save on water. They served as an artery of life to this phantasmic otherworldly Garden of Eden fallen on hard times. The trenches were deep, furrowing the ground mercilessly. They added a ravaged, bombed look to what little yard of grass there was. How I hated this elementary, ditchlike series of veins scratched out of dry earth.

Regino was scything large wheatlike weeds near the basketball backboard. Near him stood a sad and twisted apple tree that never had any hope of growing straight or tall. Nevertheless, the tree grew luxuriously. It was the only tree in the backyard that still possessed a will to live, the strength to try. The tree was propped up by a splintered and decaying two-by-four. Its branches sheltered and shaded a network of ditches that all but ruined whatever basketball playing space was available. These ditches had always caused us to stumble and fall as we bounded the ball toward the goal. The goal was low, not regulation height. Girls' height.

Regino stood under the basketball hoop, then moved the green leather hose over by the peach tree. The hot, flowing summer water cascaded from a small height into the weed-filled circle of the tree's world, muddying the parched, much too tolerant earth that bubbled with lazy insects and small summer flies.

"¿Sí, comadre?" Regino asked, looking up from his labor.

"¿No quiere un vaso de limonada, compadre?"

"¿Mande, comadre?" he said, a hand over his left ear. He was not a young man, already in his late fifties, his hearing not good, but bendito sea Dios, that was all, that was all.

"Sí, comadre, cómo no."

"¿Limonada? ¿Agua?"

"Sí, comadre, lo que sea. ¡Gracias, gracias!"

Regino bent over and vigorously pulled an unusually large specimen of plant life from the ground. It looked prehistoric, invincible, the ancestress of countless weeds, accursed mother of our present shame. The rounded ball of roots struggled to hold on. Regino held the weed aloft like a trophy. This particular life was ended. He smiled to us as we peered from the kitchen windows, and then went back to work with the scythe.

Again, Regino swooped and struggled with the clinging vegetation, little by little scything a path of his own—intent and not particularly effective.

Mercy sat on her perch by the radio. She flipped the dials back and forth, the screeching of voices and rhythms struck, now wounded the air, and hung there, suspended, full of furious, impatient life. I looked out to Regino.

"Turn that down, turn that down," Mother said, wincing. "How can you listen to that stuff?"

"Stuff?"

"Junk," she said. "Junk."

"I can't find the lemonade. Where is the lemonade?"

"Look there in the pantry, behind the clings."

"The clings?"

"Peaches."

"No, stupid, next to that thing of mincemeat."

"Mincemeat?"

"Next to the hominy!"

"I can't see it! Where?"

"There, there!"

"Oh, I forgot, there's no lemonade," Mercy said without any trace of emotion. "I finished it."

"God, Mercy, I've been looking in this stupid cabinet."

"It is *not* stupid. How many times do I have to tell you?"

"You could at least tell a person! This is what I mean, the mess! There's no lemonade, there never *was* any lemonade, and there's no ice, and the water is hot and full of watermelon seeds, and oh, I just *hate* everything!"

"Just cool it, Rocío, okay?" Mercy said, going to the door. "Maybe Toncha can come over here for her hot water."

"Funny," I said, "funny."

"Did Toncha call?"

"Oh yeah, she needs Regino."

"Why didn't you tell me, Rocío?"

"She called and I forgot."

"A long time ago?"

"Twenty minutes."

"Well, she'll just have to wait," Mother said. "At the moment, mi compadre is busy here. What's her problem?"

"Gabe," yelled Mercy.

"The water heater."

"Tell your compadre . . ."

"Can't Mercy go and . . ."

"All you do is complain," Mother whispered to herself, then louder, "Take this water to Regino."

As long as I'd known Regino Suárez, he'd been the neighborhood handyman. He did all the work the husbands never did, never could. There was always a running battle to see who would secure his services first. Even this morning Toncha Canales had called to borrow Regino to fix her water heater.

"Water heater? It's already too hot, Toncha," I thought to myself.

"You tell Regino to drop by on his way home, will you, Rocío? For some reason your mother thinks he's her personal servant. Now good-bye."

"By the way, how's Gabe?"

"Gabe," she snorted, "Gabe is Gabe. And how's your daddy? Have you heard from him?"

"My dad? Oh, not much. How's Dollie?" I asked haltingly.

"Dollie?" Toncha muttered. "Dollie is okay. How's your mama?"

"She's okay and Mercy's okay. And Ronelia, well, she's got her kids."

"Well, since everybody's okay, good-bye. Tell Regino I need some hot water! Today's my laundry day and he's neglecting this part of the street."

"So okay and good-bye."

"Who was that?" Mercy had called out.

"None of your beeswax. It was Toncha. She wants Regino to go over. Her water's out."

"So you tell him."

"I *will,* creep. How's *Goona?*"

"*Ozma* and don't bother me. I'm reading."

"You're the one who talked to me!"

"I'm reading, okay?"

And so the morning went, Mercy reading, me looking for my book, and Regino pulling weeds.

"You take this water to Regino."

From the cabinet Mother had taken the red metal glass, our oldest. She poured tap water into it.

"Go on, Rocío, take the water to mi compadre. It's so hot out there."

"Oh God, oh God, why do I always have to run these errands?"

"Now, that's enough out of you, Rocío. That's enough. I never use the word, you know I never use the word, but shut up. Shut up!"

"Okay, okay, I'll take the water."

"SHUT UP!"

"Just listen to me, Mother, you never listen."

"Rocío, I only say things once. And that's that. Ya."

"Okay, okay, so I'm going outside to take Regino his water and tell him about Toncha."

"You tell him when he finishes. When he finishes to go to Toncha's. Don't spill the water. *Where* are you going, Rocío?"

"Out the front door. I'm going out the front door. Is that okay?"

"Rocío, *what is wrong with you?*"

I held the red metal glass. Too many flies. Why wasn't the house cool? Why did someone always leave the door open? I felt the heat, saw the faraway street leading where? To town.

My eyes slid from window to window, the highest, the middle, the lowest. I could see someone outside, passing our street. He couldn't see me, but I could see him. I imagined someone coming up the winding sidewalk, an S-shaped dream, a man, and watch it, Rocío! The water is spilling!

Someone in a crowded car passed slowly down the street. I stood there with the red glass full of water, staring at the car. I was wearing my squash dress, dark green and navy blue, little squashlike patterns on the bodice and down the skirt. It was my favorite dress. It fit me well.

As I stepped into the blinding midday sun, the red metal glass grew heavier. I saw Ronald in his car, him of all people, and imagined him talking to Yolanda, the most mature, fully developed girl in the seventh grade. Ronald with his greased ducktail and tight black pants, his thick lips, vacant eyes. Ronald passed a dirty picture around the back of Miss Moran's homeroom, while Raymond Ontiveros pulled on Joanna's bra, pop it went, and the dirty picture, really the negative of

a woman in a brassiere, her flesh dark, anonymous, in luminescent underwear, fell to the scuffed floor. I stared at Ronald
as he passed in a slow-moving car. Red sun, red glass, me in
the dark squash dress. It fit me so well. Dark, lush girl in the
sunshine, seeking shade.

Oh, and now I felt dirty. Like one of Ronald's pictures. I
drank the water thoughtlessly. I stood in the front yard. No
one passed. I hurried to fill up the glass with hot clogged
water from the outside faucet.

I went around the house by the alleyway, afraid of spilling, to Regino. He had his back to me as he pulled weeds in
the farthest corner of the yard. From where I stood, I felt his
sweat. He was a small, tight man with dark rich skin like
polished cottonwood. He had no wrinkles and all his teeth.
He was born in México, but as long as I'd known him, he'd
lived in town.

I couldn't remember when I first saw him. I just remembered him doing things for us: fixing our pipes, unclogging
our toilets, laying the blue Mexican tiles in the bathroom,
body angled, crumpled, twisted, bent or flat, stick or tape or
fuse in hand, silent, industrious, easing himself always above
us on the blue, plastic-covered stepladder from the utility
room, straining toward the ceiling, the stars.

Compadre Regino never completed the sixth grade and
yet he measured, tabulated, designed, and ordered parts at
the hardware store around the corner with its sun-bleached,
stuffed bear snarling in the window, someone's testimonial
to manhood, bravery.

From the bottom of the stepladder I saw Regino's dark
armpits in his loose, white sleeves. I recalled the hardware
bear, positioned so fiercely in the sun, his reddish black fur a

fading but still powerful vision at the entryway to the hardware store: a place of gadgets, nails, rods, and tape, a place
strange and full of mysteries—men's things. Regino alone
knowing their secrets.

It was Regino who hooked up our faulty lights and tapped
the circuit breaker, teaching us in silence the eccentricities
of the television and the misbehaving vacuum cleaner. It was
Regino who hand-carried the second-party checks and who
discussed in reverential tones the best, the least expensive way
to get something done.

Regino appeared when he was needed. He was the only
one who ever emerged from the darkness to fill my father's
place. He would arrive in a dilapidated 1953 Chevy that was
usually driven by his wife, the indefatigable Braulia Suárez.

Seated next to her was her retarded daughter, Obelia, who
was fat like her mother. Pressed to the front door sat the
small, compact, and trim body of Regino, handsomely gray-
ing, with a benevolent expression of acceptance for this car-
load of his beloved obese.

Thus he would calmly arrive to help us, his other family.
The backseat was always crammed with his daughters Lorencita, Dora, Arcy, Mariquita, and Atocha. All of them had
large, expectant, bovine bodies that pressed together in an
indistinguishable clump in the Chevy's backseat.

As seen from sidewalk level, they were a wall of grinning,
ever-growing womanflesh. Regino would emerge from the
front seat, his space immediately consumed by one or another
of the backseat daughters. Obelia would then stretch out
like a purring cat, sidling up to her mother's form with a
childlike naturalness that belied her age and girth.

Braulia would pat her, gun the floorboard, and peel out

down the small street, U-turning midway in front of a passing car. The herd of girls in the back and front seats were heavy-breasted, thick-thighed, and unconcerned, indolent as well, and accustomed to full, hot meals and the fruits of their thin, wiry father's labor.

I felt Regino's sweat and approached quietly, as he might himself.

"Regino. I brought you some water."

"¡Ay!" He dropped the hoe, looked down to the grass, wiped his face with a faded, grayed handkerchief, straightened up, came closer, and apologetically took the water.

"Gracias," he said in a low voice. Regino drank the lukewarm water thirstily, as if it were a golden elixir, handed the red glass back to me, nodded gratefully, and returned to his hoe.

"De nada."

I walked quickly away. The water beaded on the rim of the glass; I could feel the wetness of the base, the gritty, sandy imprint of dusty fingers on the metal. It was a hot day, a long-drawn-out-shade-seeking summer day.

I wondered if the door was still open. When I got inside would there be shade? The squash dress was too hot in the glaring sun. It stuck to me, my thighs, my legs, my breasts. The moisture pulled the dress to me. I resolved to find that book. To find it, lie in the shade, and read, read, read.

Crossing the front yard, I sidestepped the dried, dying Willow Tree. I called at the locked door, "Mercy, Mercy, Mercy, open this door!" as the green Chevy drove up. The squash dress stuck to me in the sunlight. The car was driven by Eleiterio, Regino's only son. Handsome, handsome young man, with Regino's dark skin and bright eyes, he was the embodiment of whatever passion there was in the union between Braulia and Regino.

Eleiterio had come to take his father home for lunch. I banged on the door. "Mercy!"

Eleiterio crossed the yard, silent, dark-eyed, knowing that it was not his place as our handyman's son to speak to me.

"Mercy!"

At that moment I saw a vaporous cloud at the end of the block. It was moving down the street. An epidemic of encephalitis had prevailed that summer and the streets were turned into a war camp by the city fathers. A large truck wandered through the city streets spraying for mosquitoes. The ominous wave moved closer to me as the truck drove up.

"Let me in! Let me in the house!" Fear and dread and wild fantastic exultation overcame me in the face of the moving gray wall.

"Mercy!" I yelled. "Let me in!"

Eleiterio disappeared into the backyard. The door opened and I raced inside, sealing off the sun. I sank into the grateful semi-dark coolness of the quiet house.

Mercy was stretched on the couch reading *Ozma of Oz*. Mother was in the back room attending to her documentations of the past, going through old magazines, letters. I stared out the highest window as Regino climbed into the car. Eleiterio was at the wheel. The bright July sun was a reflecting prism down the S-shaped walk.

The green Chevy disappeared down the hot, heat-waved street, toward the mountains. Enveloped and framed in wood, I peered from the fingerprinted glass of the highest window. The shadow-crossed lawn was bordered by anxious red flowers, the zinnias that my mother loved.

I thought of the hardware bear. The heat. I felt the metal gladness of shade.

"De nada. De nada. De nada," I said.

And Mercy, "What, what?"

II

Regino Suárez and his family lived near the Old Viaduct, atop a small hill that overlooked part of Main Street, a site that in later years became the Police Department Complex. In the fall of that particular year, Regino's house faced out catty-corner to Algodones Street, which farther south led into the part of town called Little Oklahoma by certain particular and vociferous local residents who deemed the viaduct area little more than a strip of run-down secondhand stores, flea markets, and small motels of dubious reputation.

Interspersed here and there was a drive-in bar, a locksmith shop, or a greasy barbecue restaurant run by former residents of the old south who had migrated closer to the sun. In the minds of the citizenry, this new tarnished south meant gaunt, harried women with crying, mucus-crusted children and burly, monosyllabic men who had formerly worked on oil rigs and now drove trucks.

East and west were the boundaries of the town, the farms of chile and cotton. East and west were horizons of nothing but land, intimations of space now lost but still revered by the landlocked majority as part of a dying past.

North was a point beyond knowing; it led to a difference in climate, large cities, other cultures. North led to the beginnings of icy cold rivers, those streams and lakes whose water fed the crops of southern farms: cotton, red chile and green, beans and melons, alfalfa and onions. In this valley, the high cold stony peaks and mountains of snow seemed far away.

The Northern Road led to the state capital, that bastion of government, to the world of arts, to aging, fading movie stars, to their summer ranches, where the arias of art and politics intertwined.

The Northern Road led to my father, who had left his south for the crowded freedom and anonymity of the north. Like many people before him, he couldn't tolerate the heat, the blinding sun of his hometown. His was an easier world, untransformed by the slow, hot, impatient, and restless nights of incredible stillness.

And yet I wondered: did my father ever miss his hometown, the people he once loved? For to me, the southern nights were nights of waiting, nights worth waiting for, nights that heralded bright dawns in which dreams were heard and seen in the first glimmer of the daytime's moon.

Regino Suárez lived on the north side of town, where he could see the daily mechanics of a growing city on the horizon. It was a flat, open space, with great vast lots full of gray and pale yellow grass, and listless, half-dead mesquite bushes. Many of the nearby lots were litter-filled with tumbleweeds that, having blown to rest in March, still found themselves lingering in mid-October.

"*This* is what I don't like about New Mexico!" someone told my mother one day. This tourist was new to the desert, unused to the land, not yet understanding or seeing past the scrub brush and the random and disquieting disorder. "This is what I don't like," she said, pointing to one of the many weed-filled lots around the city. "It's so *messy.* Why doesn't *someone* clean it up? You would never find this back east!"

And in the midst of such a lot, now tamed, on a small, still distinct rise, facing Main Street, stood the Suárez home. The lawn was centered by a homemade cement fountain, inset with bright twinkling glass shards of pottery and colored bottles. Chickens and several dogs ran around the yard. Fluted painted metal edging was wrapped around the base of various trees. There was a small green yard to the side of the house where several bright blue metal lawn chairs were positioned in front of a tiled table, redesigned from a former cable spool.

As seen from the street, the Suárez home was large, substantial. Set away from the street—framed, as it were, by the wild, uncultivated land that surrounded it—the home was an island of labor and order and will. Regino had an eye for the smallest of details, and his home reflected and articulated beauty.

Farther north and east lay Chiva Town, where goats and pigs once roamed freely along with fowl and other domesticated animals among the brush and the desert grass. Chiva Town consisted of mostly dirt streets, crisscrossed by countless smaller ones. Within the unregistered boundaries of this neighborhood lived a portion of the town's poorest families.

Farther north and near the city park lay another world, that of the Fullertons and the Browns, black families whose sons either excelled in sports and were always winning scholarships to the state university or who were constantly in trouble with the police. So, on driving north and east from the Suárez home, one passed through parallel, but disunited worlds, worlds surrounded by invisible yet real membranes that pushed and pulled and fell back once more into themselves. They were separate, distinct, these two parts of the greater whole: Chiva Town and Brown City.

Regino's home was on the edge of Chiva Town, may one day have been in Chiva Town, but now the new elementary school and the resultant commercial development had forced the unbroken boundaries back, away from Main Street, away from Algodones Street. Regino's house was in the midst of the ever-expanding commercial sea and stood out in its unconcern for the flat, vast creeping tide of dried, materialistic life that floated to the edges of what once had been hills, what once had been farms, what once had been.

And so, carrying yet another box of used clothing, damaged mechanical devices, scuffed, stained shoes and a full pound of yellow popcorn, we arrived on Suárez Hill. The wind was blowing softly, insistently, in that October way, a portent of change. The trees, still covered with leaves, were listless, passing along responsibility to the other elements—the wind now gaining, gaining, ascendant harbinger—was mother movement of the dust-filled season. We arrived on Suárez Hill. Mercy was left behind.

Obelia rocked back and forth in one of the dark blue metal chairs that creaked with a backward push.

"Eeeeee!"

Across from her stood Zianna, the darkest, loveliest flower in the Suárez garden. A hose in hand, fingers laced over the hose head, Zianna watered the roses that grew near the street side of the house. She stood between the tame and untamed worlds, that of her father's constant laborings and that of her mother's rampant, uncontrollable life.

Zianna's face, lovely as a dark brown dusky rose, was lit with natural highlights. Her neck was long, her small, proud head balanced by a full, sensuous mouth. Her luminescent eyes shielded themselves against the elements.

Zianna had lush and firm breasts. She stood in the yard, her face in the direction of her thirsty charges. Her feet were planted firmly on the grateful grass. It was late afternoon in early autumn. The expectant air was punctuated by Obelia laughing to herself.

"Eeee!"

La comadre Nieves drove up in her dark blue Ford and called out: "Obelia, Obelia, ¡ven acá!"

Obelia ran to comadre Nieves, her large body swathed in polyester. The oversize white T-shirt bulged and strained. She appeared to be pregnant. The mercury blue marks of the lawn chairs crisscrossed her clothes. The chairs bled black-and-blue marks on the skin. The powdered paint was visible on Obelia's sausage legs and fat-filled rump.

Obelia, a merry prancing pig woman, squealed, "eee" and "ay" and "ah" and "Madrina, Madrina." Not *her* madrina, but Atocha's. Atocha and her sister piglet embraced *their* madrina, surrounding and all but obscuring she who had come to reign/rain gifts on them.

For Atocha there was a pair of white bobby socks, and for the other girls—Lorencita, Dora, Arcy, and Mariquita—scarves and handkerchiefs and faded sun hats. The summer was spent and all the offerings were dried out, heat-starched.

Obelia ran into the house with la comadre Nieves, who greeted all the girls by name.

"Ay, Madrina, Madrina!" Obelia squealed from behind the door. "¿Qué me trajiste?"

"¡Ssstt! ¡Obelia! Déjale que descanse. Sit down, comadre. Here in this chair. Aquí en esta silla. ¿No quiere un vaso de Kool-Aid, comadre? The girls just made it. Can I give you a glass?"

"Comadre, ¿no tiene una tortillita? Tengo ganas de probar de sus tortillitas tan sabrosas."

"Sí, comadre, con mucho gusto. Lorencita, bring some tortillas for my comadre Nieves. Warm them up. Comadre, they're so good with butter. Están retebuenas con mantequilla."

"Ay, comadre Braulia. Haven't you noticed I've been dieting? Gracias, Arcy, but no thank you, I don't want Kool-Aid. Can you bring me a glass of water, Dora?"

"Bring my comadre a glass of water, Dora, por favor," Braulia commanded, pulling out a chair from the red dining room set, given to her last year by comadre Nieves.

And so the boxes of clothes, socks, shoes, broken lamps, and useless watches changed hands. "Las muchachas," all of them broad, hefty girls, quietly and quickly took the cardboard boxes to their rooms. The boxes disappeared into that inner sanctum, to be ogled over later in the high excited squawking that followed a visit of la comadre's. Visits meant a new dress, a pair of shoes, a plastic bag full of circus peanuts and candied orange slices and usually, for Atocha, a small token of her madrina's love and constant devotion.

There was always something for everyone, whether it was a pair of scissors or a small broken compact mirror, filmed over with much too pale face powder, that nonetheless was intriguing, for it smelled so good, reminding the girls of la comadre Nieves, her white smooth face, her clean fragrant kindness.

Comadre Nieves visited often, especially in the summertime, when she was not teaching school and had time to go through her things, sorting clothes and old sheets, washing them and making sure they were fresh and mended. La comadre was not like other people; her clothes always came on a regular basis and they were always in the best of condition.

And she had good taste. She liked pretty things, so her bag of clothes were of the best quality. Unfortunately, Rocío and Merced were toothpick thin and only Zianna could wear their clothes. But la comadre always had other things to make up for those dresses: hats, scarves, jewelry, shoes, elastic stockings. Let Zianna have the dresses! Dora and Arcy could fit into comadre Nieves's size sixteens, and every now and then her sister in Texas sent her things. This Texas woman was the girls' size. So what if Zianna got all the Esquibel girls' dresses? What were they, anyway, but little dried sticks? And those Texas women knew how to dress!

But all this sorting out was done later, when la comadre and her daughters left the house. Usually the daughters were together, sometimes there was only one. They often stayed in the car, one of them reading in the backseat while the other sometimes came in the house and sat on the couch, looking quiet and staring at something on the other side of the room. They seemed in a hurry and were always anxious to leave.

"Mariquita!" said la comadre Nieves, eating her second-to-last tortilla. "Go tell Rocío to come inside the house, will you?"

"¡Otra tortilla, comadre?" asked comadre Braulia, her fat padded hand resting on the red Formica table top, the other busy with a dinner knife, unclogging the soiled grooves of the table's slats.

"You tell Rocío to come inside, Mariquita, that la comadre has some tortillas."

Mariquita passed through the crowded kitchen, where the muchachas all sat around eating tortillas and jam. Arcy had taken out the margarine and Dora the Bama preserves and everyone was drinking black cherry Kool-Aid with ice.

Mariquita went outside, past Zianna, who was still watering. She heard the hmmm of the water churning upward from the faucet, reeling up and dancing into the hose from the bowels of the earth and then spilling over onto the accepting earth. Mariquita felt the water in her body. She smelled the grass. What else would Zianna be doing at this time of day? Wasn't watering her pastime, anyway?

Zianna's dress was wet. She never wore pants like the other girls. She stood barefoot on the grass in a wet dress and never caught cold. She never did, she was never sick. But just maybe this time, maybe this time, thought Mariquita, she might.

"Your mother said to come inside, Rocío."

"Oh."

"She's in the kitchen."

"Oh."

"Eating tortillas."

"Oh."

★   ★   ★

I said to myself: Now go inside, Rocío. Roll up the car windows and lock the doors. And leave your book in the car this time. Go in and hurry Mother up, tell her: Mother! Remember you said we wouldn't stay long. Go inside and tell her, Remember!

The day was still warm for October, even at that time of the day when night was coming on. The car's plastic seat covers were not sticking, the little raised grooves were finally at rest, after a season of abrasion.

I was in high school, and finally becoming someone. The enveloping stillness felt good.

Why hurry? And on hurrying, where? For what?

The car was a quiet blue friend ready to take me anywhere I wanted to go: Main Street, Bob's Drive-In. I was looking for someone. Someone. That someone myself.

Later, cars full of boys passed. Once we saw Eleiterio. It *was* Eleiterio in the green Chevy.

It *was* Eleiterio, whose father was so strict, who did not allow the girls to date. Compadre Regino was an adventista. None of the girls was permitted to be seen with boys. Oh, they were content enough. On weekdays they went to school, except Obelia, who stayed home. Saturday morning there were cartoons on television, and Sunday there was church. It was all very organized. In between were meals. The girls loved to eat.

It seemed impossible to have seen Eleiterio in a passing car, alone at night, dragging Main, in that pseudo-pachuco

pretend way, but he wasn't either a pachuco or dragging
Main. I imagined things then. Almost always imagined things.
And only once or twice with Eleiterio. Su apá era adventista.

Sssmmmooosh. MMMMmmmmmm. Patter, patter, patter.
Blackbird, blackbird, what are you thinking? Zianna stood
nearby, a part of the landscape. She was too wild for the
garden's cultivation, yet too refined for the wildness of the
Suárez home. She was a small, silent blackbird on the nearest
branch.

Ssssmoooosh. Mmmmmmmm. Patter, patter, patter . . .

I imagined Zianna standing in the grass, watering, wearing the squash dress. That dress will be hers. Dark girl in the
sunshine, seeking shade.

I see myself in front of our front door. Our former front
door made of walnut, its three windows behind me like
Magi of perception: highest, middle, lowest.

How many times did I look out to see the silent street,
wait for cars to pass, and imagine faces out there, in the
darkness, coming to call for me?

The old door greeted me. Hello, familiar friend. Hello!

You are the only door I remember well. When did you
disappear? The door that replaced you was blue with intri-
cately designed wooden blocks. Regino took you away and
replaced you with another. He carried the trinity of windows to Suárez Hill, to the edge of Chiva Town. From that
vantage point life went on, catty-cornered, while las muchachas drank Kool-Aid and ate tortillas with margarine.

★   ★   ★

They laughed and talked with comadre Nieves, who knew them all by name. In the darkened living room I sat on the gray foam couch given to comadre Braulia by Toncha Canales's sister-in-law, La Minnie.

The room was half-dark in the October light. The couch was soft, too soft. The tables and the television top and the counters were clean. The wooden tables nevertheless were dry, stripped of oil. Everything in the house was old, used, secondhand, mended, fixed up, someone else's. The only things that breathed some amount of air were the plants, in coffee tins, on a peeling green table by the window. They were comadre Braulia's babies. And they were in need of water, transplanting. They lived, but halfheartedly.

"Did you call Rocío, Mariquita?"

"She's in the front room."

"Rocío! Rocío! Are you there?"

"Prende la luz, Dora, turn on that light, it's very dark in the living room."

"Mother!"

"Come and eat some tortillas."

"Take Rocío a tortilla, Arcy, por favor."

"Sí, Mamá."

"You want tortilla?"

"Thank you."

"Come to the kitchen, Rocío."

"I'm okay."

"Want some Kool-Aid?"

"I'm okay."

"What's she doing?" la comadre Nieves asked Arcy when she returned to the kitchen for a glass.

"I don't know. Looking at the door," Arcy said as she poured the drink into a red metal glass.

"Eeeeeiiiii!" Obelia laughed. "Eeeeee, el vaso, the glass is the same color as the Kool-Aid!"

"¡De veras, de veras, Obelia!" said her mother, la comadre Braulia, eating tortillas with preserves. "That's right, m'ija, it's the same color! Comadre, no quiere algo más, un taquito de carne? I can fix you some beans with chorizo," said la comadre Braulia, scratching her arm.

Mmm. Smoosh. Splash. Patter. Patter. Patter. The sound of the water on the metal chairs. Zianna is still watering. Blackbird, blackbird, what are you thinking?

III

"Ay, se fue Regino, comadre Nieves. Regino left last week and he isn't coming back."

"And why didn't you tell me, comadre Braulia?"

"I didn't tell you because I kept thinking he'd come back. Every day I prayed. The girls kept asking about him and what could I say? Your daddy's left us, he's taken up with a chorreada on the other side of town? What could I say? Arcy's birthday came and went and still no sign of her daddy. He'd taken the car or I would have sent Eleiterio over there to the puta's house to bring him back. And then today he called and asked me to put his things together and that he would pick them up later. 'Later? Later, when is later? You come home right now, Regino Suárez, you're a family man and your family needs you.' And he said, 'Vieja, I'm never coming back, except today to get my gloves that you gave me pa' Crismes and my warm socks.'

"'And what about your calzoncillos?' I asked, to which he replied, 'I have them on.'

"'Well, that's good, it has been cold, and no telling what sort of woman you've taken up with, it sounds as if her house is cold.'

"'It is,' he said, half to himself, 'but let's not talk about it anymore, you just have my things ready. Tell the girls to pack everything in the brown suitcase that I used to go to California with, to have it ready and waiting for me.'

"'Regino,' I started to say.

"'No,' he said. 'Now good-bye.'

"Well, comadre, what could I say? The girls got his things together and were waiting in the living room, but he never came inside the house. He sat in the car and honked and honked and Mariquita and Dora went out and said, 'Papá, come in!' but he didn't. He drove away without wishing Arcy feliz cumpleaños, and she cried and cried, the poor girl. That night she didn't eat her supper and you know how she loves to eat. So finally, I had to explain it to them.

"'Something has happened to your daddy. He's out of his mind, but more than that, the devil has power over him.'

"¡Ay, Diosito! I don't know him anymore, comadre! He's a changed man! So when you called me this afternoon to find out if Regino could come over and fix your TV, I thought, I'll go over and talk to mi comadre, see if she can help. Maybe you could talk to Regino and tell him to come home, comadre, to give up that pelada, whoever she is. Now why don't you show me the TV, and I'll see what I can do and then we can talk. What's wrong? The horizontal isn't working. The people on the TV are all stretched out and every once in a while they get long and then sometimes there's two of them. One of them, not the real person, but the shadow person, is usually on the left side. Is that it, comadre? The real person is usually followed by this shadow person. And it's usually worse at night, that's usually when you watch TV. How long have you had these shadows, comadre? At least a while, two weeks, a month? The shadows came on slowly, and now you get them all the time. The strange thing is that this shadow thing happened on only one channel. One channel and late at night.

"Comadre, just let me get in there and see. ¿No tiene un martillo, comadre? The last time I fixed my TV something like this happened. Except the people were short and the picture was long and in the middle of the screen. We didn't have no shadows, though. There, that's it. Comadre, I used my knife. I fixed the knob for the adjustment. It was loose. There.

"The shadows? Well, you'll just have to wait on the shadows and see if they come out tonight.

"Regino? Ay, comadre, there's nothing to tell about your compadre. He's gone. And now he's living with some desgraciada pintada chorreada and she isn't even young, comadre. I would have thought she'd be young, but no, she's not young and she's from our church! Ay, isn't that something! But anyway, she's a sinvergüenza and what does he care, puchee, as long as he has somebody to take care of him and wash his calzoncillos.

"What should we do, comadre Nieves, that's for you to tell

me. All the time I fix TVs, who says a man's the only one knows about how to do things? Ay, if there's one thing I've learned all these years, comadre, it's to take something, look at it, and fix it!"

Over Abuelita hot chocolate and sugar cookies, las comadres decided that the thing to do was to go over to that woman's house and confront her. In the daytime. That was best. That way no one could say anything against la comadre Nieves, la comadre Braulia, or los padrinos or madrinas in their party, at the confrontation con esa sinvergüenza. Also, it would be less embarrassing if by chance mi compadre was at the woman's house. God forbid, said comadre Braulia. Just as long as it was still light, because as soon as it got dark, mi compadre might be in bed in his calzoncillos, or getting ready for bed. "It could be embarrassing," comadre Braulia thought as she beat the dark rich chocolate cube with her spoon.

"No, it wouldn't be good." No telling. No telling.

She mashed the pure sweet candylike chunks in the cup of warmed milk.

No telling.

Later, on the way to la puta's in the car, Mercy and I could not believe that it was conceivably possible. Not Regino! Surely, it's a mistake!

"Now get in the car. I need witnesses," said Nieves. "We're just going to drive over there to Baca Street to la viuda Rael's, she . . . I need to talk to her about Regino. Oh, and we'll stop for Eleiterio."

"Eleiterio?" I asked.

"Eleiterio—why Eleiterio?" Mercy rejoined.

"He's going with us."

"What for?"

"To help me find her place."

"Help you, what do you mean?" Mercy asked.

"Oh, Mercy, to be there, in case . . . You know," Nieves said impatiently.

"Who is this woman?"

"A friend of mi compadre's, his . . . now will you be quiet, girls!"

"His what?"

"Friend, friend. His friend. Now be still."

South from Suárez Hill, through the narrow streets of Chiva Town with its long rows of pink and green houses bordered by metal grating from Juárez, was Baca Street and Mrs. Rael's house. It was a small, cute house with drawn curtains, a yardful of ceramic ducks and geese, a red windmill the size of a dollhouse, and bright red and blue planters with scalloped edges, like peeled-away tin cans. And there were flowers, so many flowers, zinnias, lilies, and large bushes of full-blossomed, moist-looking roses, not at all dried out as most of the town's at that time of the year.

After a bit of sisterly scuffle, Mercy planted herself by the driver's side of the backseat. I sat next to her, too close to be comfortable. On the opposite side in the back, near the door, looking anxious and compressed, sat Eleiterio Suárez.

The nights were getting colder and the plastic seats were brown and dry-looking, like the faded yellow fingers of old smokers or aged, careless diabetics. Between the seat and the seat covers were a few leaves, some dust. Only a short while ago it seemed the plastic seating had stuck to legs. Sun and sweat mingled, leaving an odor of soft secret human places

like armpits and upper arms. It was a faint aroma like the
heavy sweetness of apricots.

The smell now in the backseat was of Eleiterio, the uncon-
scious odor of a particularly aloof young man in the company
of three women. Mercy clung to the door. I clung to Mercy.
Eleiterio looked out the window, and in the front seat my
mother prayed to herself that all would go well with the viuda
whore, whoever she was. The Lord have mercy on her soul.

"Baca Street, Eleiterio?"

"815 Baca," he answered, in a short, clipped manner.

"815?"

"My dad drove me by there and showed me the house."

So! Eleiterio could speak! What he said was never of any
importance. As a matter of fact, when given a moment of
calm recollection, I never could remember the timbre or
tone of his voice. In that regard, he was like his father.

When Regino spoke, all sound stopped and out of a vacuum I felt a disconcerting moment of awkwardness. Like his
father, Eleiterio spoke with the certain halting inflection of
someone not used to speaking. His was the voice of someone usually mute, stilled in a house full of women.

In that house there was only one true voice, and it was
Regino's low, almost apologetic voice. It was matter-of-factly
correct and polite and courteous with a touch of "¿Cómo
está su papá?" and "Hello, how you been, what a pretty day!"

There was never any need for Eleiterio to speak, except
to mumble an occasional yes or no in translation. Las muchachas could giggle, and they did, repeatedly and with great
abandon whenever possible, only to be quieted and momentarily controlled by a sideways ssssst! from Braulia.

In front of la puta's, Eleiterio sat in silence looking out the car window. The sky was ocher-blue. The clouds formed a giant male with dark, staring eyes who was stretched out on his stomach with great elongated, flailing arms reaching out to a sea of vast approaching darkness. The cloud person lay on a deep blue raft, propelled through water, the small high crescent moon his only guide.

La comadre's persistent knocking could be heard, then it stopped. The silence grew inside us as outside the crickets chirped and retraced melodies in their syncopated way. Ta ta ch ch ch.

Nieves returned to the car. Mercy had opened the car door, rolled down the windows, and taken off her sweater.

"Why don't you get out, Rocío; no, here she comes."

Eleiterio looked away from the cloud man.

"No one there," la comadre said. "She's not home." All of us remembered at once the Cinderella hour of our compadre's return.

"She doesn't have a car?" Eleiterio asked from some far-away place.

"I'll come back later. Maybe tomorrow after school," said Nieves.

Nothing else was said. We drove away. As I turned back to see the rising moon, someone in the house pulled back a yellow curtain. La puta was home, waiting for her man.

"Tell your mamá we tried, Eleiterio, tell . . . You tell her we tried."

The night engulfed us in a wave of fine mist. Each day had its smells, each month, each year. Now it was apricots and roses. We heard crickets and a faraway yapping dog. And now another. They were talking to each other. We felt the hardened, aging plastic seat covers creeping up in the corners, cutting us. Our mouths were dry, our lips unmoving, as the darkened shore receded behind us. Who understands the words silence makes?

Baca Street passed by us, unlit in the narrow conduit of that flowered, trellised, sculptured world of Mrs. Rael's.

What would she and Regino want from each other but the same order, the same clarity, the same beauty? Leave them alone, leave them alone, I thought.

The town slept.

Leave them alone? There's the girls to feed, to clothe!

After twenty-five years of helping and doing things for Regino, a marriage license was of no value!

I should know, comadre Braulia thought to herself, I never got one.

"Enough you have a man, his children. What more? Let that puta desgraciada sinvergüenza chorreada vividora see if her flowers can hold him. The worst thing is that she's from the same church. So. After that, comadre Nieves, I just stopped going to church, the girls too. All except Zianna, who sings in the choir. On Sundays I listen to Oral Roberts in English. So what if his son killed himself, the father is a good man. I sing all the hymns en español.

> Jesucristo redentor
> Jesucristo mi señor

"Regino Suárez, por Dios, ¿qué te ha pasado, hombre? Like I told Arcy, 'Something terrible has happened to your daddy. He's not himself. He's a changed man.'

"Later, cuando regresó a la casa, I knew he would, I didn't ask too many questions. Better to leave it alone. When something is wrong, you just can't pretend it's right. You can go so long with closed eyes, but then one day you open them. If something is broken, well, you just have to fix it. And things can't be fixed by doing what *you* want all the time. ¡No, señor! Sometimes there's something that only *you* can do, and sometimes there's *nothing* that you can do. And if you don't do something when you *can* do it, that is, the right thing, all sorts of horrible ugly things come your way. ¡Como con esa mujer! Well, the woman's to be pitied after all. What good did all those flowers and that cute house and all her plastic animals do her? What good was the whole dirty thing, anyway, comadre? Regino already had a family. She could never have one. La pobrecita got cancer of the female kind, so that goes to show you what's right is right. Some things you can fix, some things you can't. Sometimes it's just too late. Now, I don't know about that poor woman, pero le dije a Regino, 'Viejo, if you get cancer, you can't say it was *my* fault!'

"Ay, sometimes no matter how hard you try to fix things, you can't. The Lord says, 'Ay, so now what? Do you imagine you're God or something?'

"That was all I said. It was enough. Basta. Se acabó."

IV

Nieves's fondest dream included a fountain. Regino was elected to the task, after her brief consultation with a few other builders.

"Why should I have someone else do it when I can get

Regino at half the cost with labor and supplies included? Not only that, but he's a hard worker, Rocío," Nieves said.

"When he gets down to work, and if he's on time. That's if Eleiterio or Braulia don't need the car," I said harshly.

"But he's my compadre, Rocío," Nieves replied. "A compadre is a compadre. If I can help him in any way, I'm bound by the code. Then there's the added responsibility of serving as Atocha's madrina. Besides being Regino's child, she's actually more mine now than his. Rocío, you don't understand. I'm bound by the higher laws of compadrazco, having to do with the spiritual well-being and development of one of God's creatures. Compadrazco puts me in a direct line to Heaven, that's if I respect the moral obligation of guiding the immortal soul of one of God's own. This means remembering Atocha's birthday, Christmas, and other holy days of obligation. She was given to me as a gift. She's beholden to me as I am to her.

"What if Braulia or Regino should die? Why, there's the madrina, that's me. What if Atocha were in trouble, God forbid, there's always a home, warm clothes, and food for her with me. God help a compadre or comadre if they're lazy with their duties. Even worse, God help the ahijado, if he or she forgets who his padrino or madrina are. You're the number one phone call and you'd better not forget that number. You remember that, Rocío. You could be left relationless, and what could be worse than that? You'd be disconnected from any living soul, unable to say tío, tía, or hermano.

"The warmth of a family is something you can't deny, but compadrazco is different, Rocío. It allows the best of a family's qualities to shine through. To be a compadre is to be unrelated and yet related, and yet willing to allow the relationless relation absolute freedom—within limits.

"Sometime, years before, even before you were born, Rocío, compadre Regino and I had agreed to become compadres. I had to think to myself:

1. Was I willing to hire mi compadre knowing full well the jobs could take six months, a year, be slipshod, and never to my satisfaction?
2. Was I willing to baptize Atocha, take care of her, and see if I couldn't get her a scholarship to the state university?
3. Was I willing to accept Regino's divergent religious belief and practices without a whimper, and still, in the bottom of my heart, pray for his immortal soul? You remember that shortly after Atocha's baptism, mi compadre became an adventista?
4. Was I willing to drive mi compadre anywhere, day or night, sickness or health (my own or his), that of his family, without advance warning and at the last possible moment, without so much as a murmur?
5. Finally, throughout the years, was I willing to remain constant, true, unchanging in loyalties, and despite odd behavior, unusual circumstances, and downright madness, still love, accept, and like mi compadre?

"In summary, was I willing to accept compadrazco—a union truer than family, higher than marriage, nearest of all relationships to the balanced, supportive, benevolent universal godhead? If so, I was a true comadre.

"Yes, yes, yes, yes. Yes, I said. And besides, mi compadre was a man. Tied to his maleness was the ability to do, to fix, to lift, to support, and to think through. Now, Rocío, wouldn't it be nice to have someone to *do* things around the house? When I was young that was all I wanted. Someone like my father. He was strong and he worked hard and he was there when something needed to be fixed. He didn't have any excuses. Never, not my father. Now Rocío, your father never could do things around the house, or if he could, he didn't want to. Oh, the first few years maybe, when you were little girls and I said, 'Here, hold her,' and he would. And sometimes outside, he pulled weeds and then threw them on the sidewalk, where I'd find them. Well, that was something, anyway! But then, no more. And I kept saying to myself, wouldn't it be nice to have someone around to help me? Someone to do things? Around the house. If you get married, Rocío, find someone who will help you. It makes a difference. And it's hard when you love someone who doesn't care to help. It's very hard, a painful life, really, mi'jita. All the time wishing someone would help. It's almost too much."

"But, Mother," I said, "Regino never does a decent job. Everything always falls apart and he has to fix it again. Don't you get tired of driving him back and forth?"

"He needs the work, Rocío."

"I just don't understand. Why don't you get someone dependable? Regino's been digging in the yard on and off for two weeks and all we have is a yard full of trenches. It looks like we have gophers. It's embarrassing! It reminds me of the time when Regino put up the basketball net. The same mess. The same slowness. The fountain is going to take six months.

We just finally got the tiles from Juárez and that alone took a long time. Don't you think that someone else . . ."

"He needs the work, Rocío. It'll be a pretty fountain. Just today mi compadre put in the water line. It leads from the side of the house near the willow tree to the sidewalk. All you have to do is turn it on by the faucet. But now . . ." Nieves said, "would you please clean up that toilet paper before anyone drives by. Who did that? Who wrapped toilet paper all over the rosebushes that way? Who?"

"I don't know. Someone. It was a joke."

"I wonder who did it?"

"I don't know. I guess someone wanted to play a joke."

"Get it all, Rocío!"

"¿Mande?"

"Clean it up! Oh, and don't forget to see what Regino has done!"

Spring had auspicious beginnings: days of warmth, clear sunlit stillness. After a time of peace, the wind returned, a contrary, petulant personage. It was a wind that had crossed the sea, traveled over mountains and plains, and found herself twining her undulating, pressing form between the budding trees and half-conscious shrubs of the new season. Her puffing, gesticulating, incessant labor pains were intimations of a beauty yet to be born. The hard, green-brown limbs of the rosebushes were spiked and angry still. Now they were caught and twisted in the cheapest toilet paper. The paper ran around several times, then trailed to the ground and across the dry, earth-split yard to the farthest bush, a cocoonlike larva. The tattered sheaves of two-ply fanned the air, the wind teasing them into a frenzy. On the opposite side of the yard near the driveway, Regino Suárez stood with his back to the street, shovel in hand, burrowing down to clear a path for the water line. He was nearly done with this part of the work, and he felt content. The work was going well.

I jumped over the sidewalk and began the process of stripping the bushes. The toilet paper stuck to the sharp thorns or floated away in the insistent, slightly chilled wind. When would summer come? I thought. When will we be done with this wind, this wind, this wind that doesn't stop?

A foot of filmy paper flew across the yard and into Regino's path. He picked it up and, dexterously moving through the broken ground, sidestepped his way to me. He handed me the paper.

"The paper, it blowed to me."

"Thank you, Regino," I said, stuffing it into a paper-filled fist.

"I saw the paper and I said to myself, 'Regino, what's this?' Pretty funny, ¿qué no?" He chuckled to himself, lifting off a few squares from the nearest branch. "It's the paper for the toilet."

"Yes, it's kinda silly."

"Pretty funny."

"Mamá was mad at *me*. I didn't do it."

"El excusado," he said to himself, laughing shyly.

"Yes, it's pretty funny. Somebody did it as a joke."

"The kids, eh?"

"Mamá wasn't happy."

"¡Ay, qué los chamacos!"

Regino peeled off another square of the paper and put it in his shirt pocket.

"¿Cómo está su apá?" he said, more seriously.

"Oh, he's okay."

"He's always the same. Ah, qué mi compadre. But he doesn't know what's good for him. Pobrecita de mi comadre. Always waiting for your daddy to come home. Ah, qué mi compadre, he's lucky, if only he knew it. Your mamá, she's a good woman. Mi comadre loves the Lord and He loves her. He's the only one who's gonna bring your daddy back home. You take care of your mamá, Rocío, and the Lord will take care of you. The Lord has taken care of me and I'm an old man. I'm not too old yet, but I'm getting older. And so is your mamá. You need some help with the paper?"

"No, Regino, thank you."

"The work is good," he said, pointing to the dug-out yard and the shiny new water line. "See, here's a drawing of the fountain, the water's going to come out of the top, and in the middle is this bath for the birds."

"It's very nice, Regino," I commented, looking at the crude drawing. It showed a blue-tiled bowl, from which a small spout emitted a high steady stream of water. The statue of Saint Francis would come later.

The tile was from Juárez, from La Casa de Oppenheimer. Before the fountain came the tiled basin in the bathroom. The fountain was an afterthought.

I stared at the creased, softened paper, the pencil markings detailing more than just a tiled fountain. Could I gauge the part of Regino that went into that beloved fountain of my mother's? It was a creative act of his, and yes, the fountain would be lovely, for as long as it would last.

★   ★   ★

The water was the chief problem, there was either too much or too little. The fountain switch sent up an enormous jet straight into the air. Two people were needed to monitor it, one to turn on the switch, the other to report on the water's height. The fountain, as a result, was rarely in use. It was a "company" fountain, a quiet, late-in-the-afternoon fountain. It had a pleasant tinkling sound and was loved by all the birds who bathed in it. With a dark rush of softened wings, they flew away refreshed. From behind the door Nieves stood watching the birds bathe themselves in the late afternoon of a windy spring day.

"Turn the fountain down! Turn it down! And roll up the car windows!"

Sometimes Nieves sat on the small concrete porch or on one of the metallic blue lawn chairs and thought: How nice it would be to have someone around. Someone to help me. Do things. All my life I've looked for someone. Well, it's quiet now, except for the crickets.

"Turn the fountain on. What Rocío? Going out? Nooo-oo! Why don't you stay home? Higher. Turn it higher. Too high. Lower. Lowerrr . . . No, higher. And where are you going? Did you clean the kitchen? Are you coming home early? Rocío, just *who* spread that toilet paper? Was it someone I know? Leave the fountain on now, I'm just going to sit here in the dark. I'm okay. We need a new statue of Saint Francis. Higher. Fix the plastic statue there in the middle. The birds, they like it. I just don't understand *who* would do such a thing. I came outside and my Saint Francis had on an orange life preserver. Why can't you stay home? Where are you going? M'ija, leave the fountain on and *don't* come in late. Who could it have been, Rocío? Who? Someone you know? No, that's too high. Lower. There. Now listen. Can you hear the birds?"

V

"Somebody's at the door, Mrs. Esquibel. There's someone at the door! Rocío, come and get it. Damn it, stop ringing. What the hell?" Salvador Esquibel said in a booming voice on one of his few visits home.

"Compadre Salvador!"

"How have you been, Regino?"

"Buenas tardes, compadre."

"Pásale, come on inside."

"Nomás quería preguntarle a mi comadre Nieves alguna cosita, compadre."

"Hot out there? Qué calor, ¿qué no?"

"You look good, compadre Salvador."

"I feel pretty good, Regino."

"Still living up north?"

"Yes."

"You look real good."

"I feel pretty good."

"Qué gusto verlo, compadre Salvador. Hace muchos años que . . ."

"Time sure flies, eh?"

"We're getting old, compadre."

"Not me. I feel good as ever. And you?"

"It's the Lord. He's given me good health, a family, and all my teeth, compadre. Who needs anything else?"

"You want to talk to Nieves?"

"Sí, compadre, por favor."

"Nieves! Nieves! Rocío, call your mother. Rocío! God damn, where are all those women?"

"The Lord has sustained me, compadre. He's the only one. All these years of hard work and I'm still in good health. ¡Gracias a Dios! Oh, I got crazy once, compadre. It was Satan. He entered my heart. But no more. Since then I've been working for the Lord."

"Nieves! Damn it, where is she?"

"Did you call, Daddy? Oh. Buenas tardes, Regino."

"Buenas tardes, Rocío. ¡Ay, qué muchacha tan bonita! She's a pretty girl, just like her mother. Sí, compadre, debiera estar muy orgulloso de las muchachas."

"Their mother's done a good job."

"Ay, mi comadre es una santa. She's a good woman."

"Nieves! Regino's here. Dammit, where's your mother?"

"She's in the backyard, watering."

"Watering, dammit, at this time of the day?"

"I'll go and call her."

"Yes, Rocío's a good girl. She's a teacher."

"Ay, qué bueno. Cómo me da gusto ver a una familia junta. ¿Y el baby? ¿Se casó?"

"Did you say something, compadre?"

"¡Que Dios los bendiga, compadre. Y les guíe por esos caminos oscuros, que Dios los bendiga, compadre, may God bless and protect you."

"Here comes Nieves!"

"Usted se ve muy bien, compadre Salvador. You look very good."

"I feel pretty good. No complaints, oh no, not Sal . . ."

"Ay, comadre Nieves . . . ¿cómo está?"

"Compadre Regino, sit down."

"Comadre, ¿qué le pasó al water main? Did the water main break?"

"When did you get here, compadre? Has it been long? Who brought you?"

"Por chanza me dieron ride, comadre. One of my friends gave me a ride. Excuse me, but I'm going outside to see the main. Comadre, con permiso. Compadre, con su permiso."

"Sure, you go right ahead, Regino."

"Excuse me. It's so good to see you all together. Your daddy says you're a teacher, Rocío. What about the baby? And your other sister?"

"Mercy's married and has two children. And Ronelia, she's got six."

"That's real good. Compadre, it's been a pleasure. I'm so happy to see you again. The Lord bless you."

"Gracias, compadre."

"Come this way, compadre."

"Sí, comadre. Ay voy. Here I come."

There was a silence and then a pause.

"When did Regino become so religious, Rocío? What is he, a priest?" asked Salvador.

I could hear noises from outside: a faraway bark and high-pitched voice under the hum of a distant lawn mower.

"Damn, Rocío, did you see Regino's suit? Damn your

mother; that's my old brown suit! She gave it to him! The last time I was here I brought some laundry, and after I got back home half of it was missing. She gave it to him, and not only that, but he was wearing my tie. Can you believe your mother? She'll strip you naked and give your clothes away to Regino Suárez and his family."

"*That* was your suit?"

"My old brown suit. I really liked it. It had a few years left."

We sat in the silence of a room full of marbled shadows of hair and arm and window frame. The air was hot and still, full of unvoiced exasperation. Our emotions were twisted, they whirled and danced in the unrelenting wind. Each of us felt alone, with the insidious seeds of vague, unnameable discontent. We looked away from each other. Outside voices hummed, birds sang, and the trees' shadows lengthened. It was 5 P.M. on a Sunday afternoon in July. Now and then a firecracker went off, slicing the arid and empty air with token significance.

"Damn, Rocío! Did you see Regino's suit? Damn your mother, that's my old brown suit! You can't bring anything into this house or it gets lost."

The wind subsided.

"Last summer I left a box of shoes here and now they're lost."

"She probably gave them to Regino."

"I don't know. I still think someday I'll find them. Who knows when."

Nieves Esquibel entered from outside. She looked flushed, the bottom half of her cheeks dotted with red.

"Nieves! Regino was wearing my old suit and my tie!"

"Sssshh! He'll hear you. I know it!"

"It was my favorite suit!"

"It was old and ugly. You of all people deserve nicer clothing. And the tie had cigarette burns and you told me you stopped. . . ."

"*He's* wearing the tie, it's okay for him."

"I cleaned and sewed the clothes."

"The suit had a few years left."

"Mr. Esquibel, a man of your position deserves a better wardrobe."

"Mother, by the way, did you ever find my shoes?"

"What shoes?"

"The ones I left here last summer. They were in a box, about six pairs of shoes."

"You never left any shoes here, Rocío."

"See what I mean? They're lost."

"What are you talking about, Rocío?"

"Don't be so touchy, Nieves. Rocío, your mother can never crack a smile."

"I'm not touchy. It's you who's touchy. You can't be here five minutes without blaming me for something."

"Damn!"

"No, you don't! You're not going to blame me or anyone else for your foul mood."

"Foul mood! Dammit, I feel good!"

"See how he torments me, Rocío."

"Oh, just stop it!"

"Not until he apologizes."

"For what?"

"See how he is?"

"Damn, I knew I shouldn't have come, Rocío. I don't care

if it is July the fourth. Every time I come back, it's the same thing, the same arguments."

"There you go again, Salvador."

"I don't care."

"Don't you threaten me."

"I'm not threatening you, Nieves. It's just that I didn't come back here to take your . . . your . . ."

"Mamá, please don't cry."

"I'm leaving tonight."

"See, see, always threatening."

"My head hurts."

"So does mine."

"You think it's so goddamn easy."

"Please, please."

"Oh stop crying, Nieves, dammit!"

There was a knock at the door. It was Regino. Salvador cleared his throat and Nieves wiped her eyes.

"Oh, comadre, comadre . . ."

"Un momento, compadre."

"That's my goddamn suit, Nieves!"

"I know it! I know it! What do you want me to do?"

"That's my favorite goddamn suit!"

"You have so many suits. What's one old baggy, stained, beaten-up, ugly brown suit? And besides, it was a winter suit."

"I wore that suit last summer."

"Please."

"So why's he wearing it?"

"Sssh! He'll hear you."

"I knew I shouldn't have come, Rocío. Your mother gets this way every time I come here. That's why I don't come to visit more often. I'd like to come and visit. This *is* my hometown. My mother and all my brothers and sisters live here, but Rocío, I just can't take it. You understand, don't you?"

"Mi compadre needs a ride, Rocío. Why don't you take him in your car?"

"We'll take him; come on, Rocío. Let's get some fresh air."

"Don't you want to eat supper, darling?"

"It's too early for supper. We're not hungry now. We'll eat later when we come back. Okay, Nieves?"

"Okay, Mamá, we'll be right back."

"Come back soon. I want to go to Morales Park and see the fireworks at eight o'clock."

"What? Fireworks? What fireworks?"

"Does Regino live in the same place, Nieves, over there by Algodones Street?"

"Oh no, he moved years ago. He lives close to the new junior high, Piñónes, over there by your uncle Lino's."

"Up there? When did he move up there?"

"Years ago."

"What's up there?"

"Houses."

"Houses I know. What's up there that he lives up there?"

"Government houses. They're very nice."

"How long have the wetbacks been allowed up there on the hill?"

"He's not a wetback. If you'd come back more often to see your mother . . ."

"There you go again, Nieves."

"Your uncle Lino is very sick, Salvador. He's dying. When

was the last time you saw him? He always asks for you. On your way back you can stop and see him. Rocío knows where he lives."

"Now just . . . Damn! Nieves, I'm just going with Rocío to take Regino. I don't want to see Tío Lino today."

"He's dying. He'll die and then you'll be sorry. But come right back. The park will get filled up and we have to eat!"

"So then how can we stop to see Tío Lino?"

"Just stop."

"Compadre Regino, ¿ya está listo?"

"Sí, comadre, gracias."

Later, on the way back from taking Regino home, Salvador asked, "Since when do people on welfare live in two-story houses?"

"I don't know, Daddy."

"Damn! It's a mansion! It pays to be on welfare these days. How many kids he got?"

"I don't know."

"Regino Suárez lives in that two-story house and pays $25 a month rent, all utilities?"

"Seventy-five."

"How many kids he got?"

"Zianna married a soldier from the base and moved to Montana and the boy, Eleiterio, got sent to Vietnam, and the others, they stay home."

"Damn, it pays to be on welfare!"

"I was on welfare once."

"Christ, your mother never tells me anything. She's always

quiet about things, so I have to ask *you*. Regino lives in that house? Hmmmm . . . that big pretty house?"

"It's very nice inside."

"He's still with the fat wife?"

"They got married."

"And the retarded girl?"

"She works at one of the high schools."

"It's hard to believe that those houses are low-rent, when there was nothing up there but dirt hills before."

"Uncle Lino's house?"

"No, I want to go home. I mean, to your mother's. Take a nap. And anyway, he depresses me."

"What about Morales Park? I was . . . going out . . . with a friend. . . ."

"I'll go and see Uncle Lino tomorrow when I feel better. The last time I saw him all he did was cry. Since when do poor Mexicans live like kings in two-story houses? Christ, it's a mansion! Rocío, you take your mother to the park. It's July Fourth, take her to the park!"

"There'll be fireworks. Don't you want to go?"

"I know, I know, but I'm tired. I can't be doing everything with her. We *are* divorced."

"It's July Fourth."

"Independence Day. You take her!"

"Why are you laughing?"

"Christ, it was my favorite suit!"

"That one?"

"Your mother, Rocío, she's a character!"

"Yes, I know."

"Where is it that Tío Lino lives?"

"We passed it already."

"All he does is cry."

"Yeah."

"I'll go and see him tomorrow. ¡Ah, qué mi tío Lino! I never thought the day would come when that damn wetback would be living up there by my tío's in that mansion! Rocío, we'll go up there tomorrow, what do you say?"

"I'll think about it tomorrow."

"What did you say?"

"Gone with the Wind."

"Oh. We'll go up and pay him a visit. We'll go up there and pay him a visit. Christ, I never did think that Regino would be up there in a mansion with Tío Lino dying around the corner. Did your mother say he was dying?"

"They're starting."

"What?"

"The fireworks."

"Since the morning, Rocío, it's been that way. It's always that way. Baby, let me tell you, I'm never coming back. It's your mother. She gets that way. Goddamn firecrackers!"

VI

When it's autumn, it should be winter, and when it's winter, we wonder about spring. We think we remember the seasons. But we don't remember the temperature, the way the air moved, how the moon looked, and how we carried our sorrows with us, bundled up in what passed for pleasures, activities, plans.

It was autumn, but winter was the true season. And in

that brisk clarity of that shortened parade of dreams, winter held us close.

Regino stood to the side of the S-shaped walk, which was now cracked and furrowed by grass. The lilies on either side of the walk were stunted, with dried yellow edges. The weeds jutted between the spent flowers and called attention to themselves. They were fierce, deep-rooted, and simply refused to be vanquished.

"Hierbas, hierbas, hierbas! Bend over, pull now, pull again and stop. Look around and wonder if mi comadre will take me home soon. If I had a car, I would go by myself. But to have a car you must have a family. And to have a family means to have people around to feed. To have a car is to worry. And I don't want to worry anymore. Let the Lord take care of everything.

"When Braulia and the girls left me, my heart was hard, a piece of rock that had lain in the sun too long. Yet there was a detachment. So when Braulia called to say, 'Mariquita's gotten pregnant and she wants to keep the baby and live at home, just like she always has,' I was far away. Far away, soaring.

"Braulia couldn't understand that. And I thought, you too, Braulia, are soaring! You left me, you and the girls. And it's good. You've always been like blackbirds, cawing, cawing, and eating all the crumbs. Go on, fly, fly! And then I thought: It was you, Braulia, who decided to move to Montana, to leave me here.

"Now Mariquita is pregnant, Zianna is having trouble with her boss, and Eleiterio is breaking up with his wife and into the drink. Go on, let him, I say! No one has the right to stop anyone from killing themselves if that's what they want to do. Nobody has the right to stop suffering if people want to suffer. Let him go through it, Braulia. Let him get low and them come crawling back into himself and the darkness within him like I did.

"Then maybe he'll be able to love. And you thought I was going to say live. What is living without love? Go on, let him. And when you go through so much, as I have, little things fall away, and if everyone were to leave you alone, in a place by yourself, like me, in my duplex, and you had no car to get anywhere, why there wouldn't be anywhere to go, or nobody to see unless you wanted to see them.

"And then all you had to do was look around and the Lord would show you things: places and people out there, and He would provide food, friends, new slippers like the ones comadre Nieves gave me for my saint's day, and a car, and if not a car, a ride.

"So when Braulia asked, 'Don't you care?' I said yes and no. No, I don't care anymore and yes, I care more than ever. But not about you, but about everything and everyone. Oh yes, I care! Somewhere far away and somewhere very close.

"And this comes through suffering. Only through suffering. So leave the chamacos alone—let them figure it out, and do report it to me, vieja. I still like to hear the stories.

"'You stubborn old man,' she said. 'You couldn't come to Montana with your family, could you? You had to stay there!'

"No, I said, after all these years, this is my home. You don't understand, do you, vieja, what order is, and peace? Order is going home to my brown slippers with the wool inside. Order is taking off my work boots and fixing a bit of food. Oh, I don't eat much anymore. I wash my dish and my spoon and my fork. I drink my Sanka and then I go outside my duplex. It's really nice, vieja. It's by the new junior high school, one bedroom, a duplex, me dijeron, that's what they call that kind of place. And it's paid for by the government.

"Peace is sitting on the metal chair that I kept—I hope you didn't sell the others, vieja, and if you did, don't tell me. Peace is sitting out there watching the trees move and feeling the wind. And it's not feeling sad anymore, because you want people to be this or that way, and you want this or that thing and the flesh is okay, but there's nothing, vieja, like the quiet afternoons when I sit in my chair. I look at the fountain. It's like the one I made for la comadre Nieves.

"I don't think about anything, vieja, not even the flesh. No, there's peace, peace and love. For no names and for nothing in particular. I look around me and I think of you. And you are part of this rainbow, vieja. In this dream of mine. I looked up and you were a light in the sky. A white rainbow.

"But then you said, 'But a rainbow doesn't have white light, and besides, what a way to think about your wife! And I am your wife, because you finally married me, pendejo! Some husband you are! Okay, keep your white lights and don't move to Montana! Me, I want to see things, to live, and so do your children. They want to live, too. They want a new life, a real life. They want and need the world. ¡Ay, qué loco! A white rainbow in the sky. Only *you* would say that, that's the way it is with you, loco!'

"'That's the way it is,' I said to her out there in the darkness. In front of my duplex. Let them live! Let them see the world! Go on, fly! You, Braulia, up there in the sky! You don't understand, do you? And even that passed away."

★   ★   ★

"¡Ay, estas hierbas malditas! Mi comadre will come and take me home. I'll come back tomorrow and finish the work. Maybe I can get some of the chamacos in the neighborhood to come and help me pull these weeds. I guess I'm getting old. They need the money, esos chamacos flojos! They can come to la comadre's and I'll tell them what to do. Me, I don't need much money now. Stop now and pull. Stop and look around. Rest.

"When I get home I can warm up that soup que me dio la comadre Nieves y esas tortillas. I'll have my Sanka. I'll do the dishes and then I'll sit outside and watch the sky. Pull and stop. Pull and stop.

"Yes," I said, straightening up. "I'm getting old. I may be old, but I'm not a viejito. There *is* a difference.

"Ay, I'll go home now. I'll come back tomorrow and finish estas hierbas malditas! I'll come back, you tell my comadre Nieves not to get anyone else. I'll come back and finish later. . . . I'll come back . . . and finish . . . later. ¿Bueno? Okay!"

"What are you giving Regino for his birthday, Mother?" I asked. We were in a car.

"A bathrobe, Rocío, to go with his slippers."

"The same one you gave Daddy?"

"They were on sale and your dad will never know."

"Does Regino wear the slippers?"

"Yes."

"How is he? Where does he live?"

"Alone. Braulia and the girls moved to Montana to be

close to Zianna and her husband. She married a soldier from the base."

"And Eleiterio?"

"I don't know, he got married, has a baby."

"But Regino . . ."

"They left him alone, his family left him alone."

"And isn't he lonely?"

"Yes, he was, but I said, 'Compadre, you're better off now. All you did was worry about the girls.' The girls wanted to date, but he wouldn't let them. He was too strict. They moved away so they could date. Oh, they wanted him to go with them but 'No,' he said, 'this is my home.'"

"He must be so lonely."

"Yes. But later on, he said to me: 'You were right, comadre, the Lord had given me peace of mind, just like you with compadre Salvador. Praise God. Praise God.'"

"I don't know," I said. "It seems so hard for them to have left him, that way. So hard."

"Oh, he's better off. But yes, it's hard, Rocío. It's very hard. It's hard for me, everyone gone. But I have peace of mind. I have peace of mind now. It's taken so long, so long."

"Just the same . . ."

"No, Regino's all right. And don't you worry about me. I'll be okay."

"How's your family?" I started to ask Regino the next time I saw him, but then I stopped. "How's your new place?" I asked instead.

It was late morning. Regino was out in the front yard

pulling weeds. He was still handsome, still had a mouthful of teeth, but now he was stooped, slightly breathless.

"It's the heat," he said, trying to account for his tiredness. He stood solemnly, wiping a sweat-filled brow. "It's so hot."

"That never changes," I said, and looked away and then back.

"Your mamá," he said, "she's not well. I had this dream, Rocío. All she needs is to have you girls come back home and she comes to life. She's always busy with things, but when you are here, she comes to life again. I had this dream, Rocío. I don't know, it's good to see her come to life again."

Regino propped his hand on the upraised hoe.

"Ay, that's all for today."

VII

"Compadre Regino, I want you to meet my brother, Roque, and his son, Tommy," Nieves said. "This is my compadre, Regino Suárez, Roque. Pase pa' dentro, compadre. Come in. Roque quiere comprar unos tamales, and I told him that you had a compadre who makes tamales at the factory, La Buena."

"Sí, comadre, cómo no. La comadre Nieves baptized my daughter Atocha," he said to Roque.

Later Roque and Regino sat on the living room couch talking about the weather, tamales, and the merits of California. One year Regino had picked fruit up by Bakersfield.

"It was a happy time," he said wistfully, sitting on the edge of the dark blue sofa. Regino never sat back fully; he was always perched on the edge of the chair or couch, ready to jump up, spring forward, take off in any given direction. When I entered the room, freshly made up, dressed in a white blouse and a long cotton skirt, Regino rose.

"Rocío!"

"Tío Roque! Tommy! How are you and when did you get in?"

"A little while ago, chula."

"Dios la bendiga, Rocío. God bless you and keep you. ¿Cómo está?"

"Muy bien, compadre. How is your . . . apartment?"

Stop. Stop and pull. Now rest.

"We're going for tamales, Rocito. Do you want to come with us, pretty girl?" Roque asked.

"¿Adónde van, tío?"

"The tortilla factory."

"To get tamales," Tommy said.

"They sell tamales? I didn't know that."

"Sí," said Regino. "My compadre Wecesalo makes them."

"Nieves, hermana, leave everything. We're going for tamales!"

"Can we all fit in the car, Papi?"

"Hell yes, Tommy."

"Ah, qué Roque, fíjate, compadre. ¡Este panzón barbón es el baby! ¡Es el baby de la familia!"

"Eeeeh, qué baby tan feo!" said Roque.

"Ay no, Señor Roque," insisted Regino.

"Yes, I am the baby of the family," he said, proudly stroking his enormous stomach.

"So let's go, Dad. You get in the back with mi tía Nieves and Rocío, and Regino and I will sit up front, para que me dirija, compadre. You can tell me where to go, eh?"

"Oh, no," compadre Regino protested. "Yo me siento atrás. Please let me sit in the back."

"Compadre, siéntese adelante con m'ijo. And that's that. Are we in? Nalgas listas?"

"Can we all fit?" Nieves said, giggling like a schoolgirl at her brother's joke. I sat in the middle, between the fat and aging joyful brother and sister.

"¡Es el baby, compadre Regino!" Nieves laughed.

"¡Ay, qué baby tan feo!" Roque repeated. "I'm the ugliest baby you ever saw!"

"Mi baby acaba de graduar con su B.A.," Roque said proudly.

"Graduated cum laude," Tommy said. "She's a good student. And I'm not only saying this because she's my sister."

"¿Usted no tiene familia, compadre Suárez?" Tío Roque asked with respect. "Tell me about your family, compadre."

"Now, then, Roque was the baby, compadre," Nieves said, "then there was Alicia and Manuel. And then the others. They're gone now. That's four of them. And Mom and Dad. All gone."

We drove down the familiar, once small and magical east-facing street to La Buena and the tamales that would find their way to Tío Roque's house in Ventura, to Tío Roque's wife and his two educated children, one with a B.A. in home ec, the other with an M.A. in business.

Good-bye to the street and hello to Chiva Town. La Buena Tortilla Factory.

"I'll go inside and talk to mi compadre," Regino said. "I'll get the tamales."

"Here's some money, compadre."

"I'll be right back."

"And so what do *you* do?" Tommy asked, turning to me in the backseat. "I hear you write."

"She's a famous Writer," Tío Roque said as we waited for the tamales. "Or she will be. Aren't you a Writer, Rocío?"

"Yes," I said, "I write. I'm a writer."

"He was such a pretty baby, Rocío," Nieves said, patting her brother's grayed head. "So pretty, with big, bright eyes and huge beautiful eyelashes. Everyone thought he was a girl."

"¡Ay, qué Nieves!"

"He was a pretty baby, Rocío, and now look at the canas! Just look at all that gray hair!"

"No, Nievesita. I'm not a baby anymore. Tommy, you help compadre Regino with the tamales."

"¡Estoy bien! I'm fine. I can carry them!"

"Regino's getting old, Rocío. Have you noticed?"

"Yes, I have."

"His family lives in Montana," Nieves said to her brother.

"He just can't work as hard as he used to and tires easily. But I still give him jobs."

"I noticed he redid the door, Mother."

"What, Rocío, do you like it?"

No, no, I thought. It's ugly. I don't want you to be afraid. If you're afraid, I will be too. Take off the metal bars and bring back the trinity.

"Donacio, the new man, he did the work."

"The screen door is coming apart and . . ."

"Oh, I know. I know. There's so much to do! Rocío, and no one to help me. No one to do it. All I ever wanted was for someone to help me."

"When did you get the new door?"

"Oh, it's been a while. Don't you like it?"

"Eh, Papi, ¡están calientitos! Pero de veras!" shrieked Tommy. "Watch it, the tamales are really hot!"

"¡Tamales de La Buena! ¡Qué treat! We're going to take them home to Califas with us, compadre."

"Bakersfield?"

"Ventura, compadre. Ventura."

"¿Por dónde queda Ventura? Where is it? Is it close to Bakersfield?" Regino asked.

"Here, Tommy, let me hold them."

"I got them."

"Okay, Writer, now hold those tamales."

"Did you fix the door?" I asked Regino earlier that morning, pointing to the dark metal grating that outlined the front door. It was clumsy work, and it clanged and banged each time someone opened or closed the door. The blue metal was oversized, ominous, repelling easy entry. It was the door to a fortress now, where Nieves locked herself in, afraid of strangers, herself a stranger. Afraid. All the windows, too, were covered with the dark blue ironwork that blocked any lingering view from the outside world.

"Oh no," he said, "your mother's other man, Donacio. He did it."

"Donacio?" I said with surprise.

"He's a primo from Tejas."

Later we sat down to eat hot tamales. It was the first time Regino and I had ever sat down together.

"Siéntase, compadre. Everybody sit down to eat! Vamos a probar los tamales. Echame unos calientitos, Tommy. Get me a hot one from the bottom, son. Now pass the plate to compadre Regino. Now Nieves and the Writer."

"¿No quiere algo de tomar, compadre?" I asked. "What would you like to drink? Juice? Milk? Water?"

"He can't hear you, Rocío. Speak louder," Nieves whispered.

"No quiere algo de tomar?"

"Louder. Just give him a glass of water, Rocío."

"Nomás un tamal, por favor. I don't eat much. One tamal will do. Gracias, comadre."

"Gracias a usted, compadre."

"He's ready to say grace, Rocío, wait."

"Divino Pastor, le doy gracias por este día de tantas bendiciones, por la comida, por el sol, por el trabajo, y especialmente por el amor que se difusa y se ve en estas caras, las caras de tus hijos. We have so much to be thankful for, Divine Father, but most especially for the love in this family. Que aquí están celebrando los misterios de tu divina vida y muerte. Le damos gracias, Señor Jesucristo Redentor, y le pedimos que nos dé la fortaleza para que podamos servirle con todos nuestros corazones, ahora y en adelante. Make us strong, Father, so we can serve you in this life and in the next. For only you know what our life and death will be. Amen."

"¿Otro tamal, compadre? Would you like another tamal?"

"¿Mande?"

"I don't think he can hear you. Just give him another tamal."

"Echame otro, Tommy. Pass them around, son. So, where's Mercy?" Tío Roque asked, unshucking a green chile cheese tamal.

"She lives up north. Me, too. Somehow it just happened."

"I miss them, Roque. I miss my girls," Nieves said sadly.

"Mamás! They never give up, do they, Rocío?"

"No, I never will, Roque. Never. Someday my girls will come home."

"¿Más jugo, compadre? Oh, I mean more water?"

"¡Qué tamales tan ricos!"

"They're pretty good!"

"It's a feast! And we still have some to take home to your mother, Tommy!"

"So what do you do, Rocío?" Roque said. "I mean, can you make a living? What do you write?"

"Oh, about people. New Mexico. You know, everything."

"I tell her, Roque, to write just one *Gone with the Wind*. I say, Rocío, just write about this little street of ours. It's only one block long, but there's so many stories. Too many stories! And then I thought to myself, but why write about this street? Oh, there's Toncha and Gabe and Manuelita Acevedo at the other end with her ugly little dog, and across from her is La Prieta Armendáriz and her flowers, but why write about this street? There's stories all right, but why write about this street?

"Why not just write about 325? That's our house! Write about 325 and that will take the rest of your life. Believe me, Rocío, *at least* the rest of your life. Just write about this house. There's you and your daddy, que Dios lo cuide, and Mercy and her kids, and Ronelia and her kids, and me, don't forget *me*! I could have my own book!

"I tell her, Roque, just write one *Gone with the Wind*. That's all. Just one. You don't have to go anywhere. Not down the street. Not even out of this house. There's stories, plenty of them all around. What do you say, Rocío?"

"Más tamales, anybody?" I said. "Compadre?"

¡ M I L   G R A C I A S !

This book is a celebration of many lives. Through it I can tell my parents how much I love them. And in the telling, they are always near to me. They should be remembered as much for their gift of humor as for their great storytelling skills. They were my first teachers and knew a good punch line when they said one.

Thank you to Delfina Rede Faver Chávez, who was my best friend and first critic. She was a far-seeing, ever-loving guide who gave me my first copy of *Soule's Dictionary of English Synonyms* with the inscription "To a future great writer on her 12th birthday, my love and blessings, Mother." She kept me in dictionaries, pens, paper, and diaries enough to last a lifetime, and her last gift to me was a collection of short stories she thought I'd enjoy. My father, Epifanio Ernesto "E.E." Chávez, gave me books galore because I loved them and allowed me to make library cards for all the books in his extensive library without saying a peep. Daddy was an irascible human spirit, a man of great intelligence and charm, a Jack Benny to my mother's Lucille Ball.

For the great blessing of friends who have come and gone I am thankful to: Constance Marie Gale, Dan Turner, Lloyd Watts, Mark Stevenson, Annie Winkle, Louie Estrada, Jim Donohue, Bill Frankfather, Hershel Zohn, and José Quintero, as well as my dear brother-in-law, Michel Charles. And of course, who will ever forget José García, el compadre, who was a father figure to all of us in the 'hood and passed away at age one hundred not so long ago. May they all rest in peace!

My sisters, Margo Chávez-Charles and Faride Conway, love books as much as I do and they are my true literary kin. They have made my life immensely rich—both in and out of story.

I want to thank Kevin Kelly for his enormous loving heart and larger-than-life presence. My blessings to Bill Coleman. Someday I promise you I'll write *that* story.

For years of support I have many people to salute: Rudolfo Anaya, my first editor, my friend, my writing compadre. He was the first person who looked me coldly in the eye and challenged me with "So, what are you going to do with your life? Are you going to be a writer, or what?"

Along with Rudy, there is his wife, Patricia, who is a sister in spirit.

My agent, Susan Bergholz, has encouraged me to revisit Rocío's world with fresh eyes after all these years and has offered insight and support. My editor, Alice van Straalen, has laughed soundly at all of my jokes and followed me down every circuitous path, sideswiping many a dust devil to spur me on to do my best work. Her thoughtfulness and care have been a blessing.

I can't forget Mary Jean Haberman, my housemate in Albuquerque, who took me in that long hard year when I was at the University of New Mexico. She rented me a room in her lovely home and shared many a goulash with me. Those wild and spontaneous meals nourished and sustained me in those crazy days. We had so much fun, Mary Jean! You made me laugh even when I was sick as a dog and trying to become the writer I knew I was. I will always hold you in my heart, comadre.

Kenneth Kuffner, my lawyer for many years, took me on and wouldn't let me go. He believed in me as the tides ebbed and flowed. There's no way I can repay him for his generosity and assistance through that long marathon that was our legal collaboration.

Friends in the literary community supported me as well during the hard years and remain special to me: Gary Soto, Sandra Cisneros, Susan J. Tweit, Sandra Benítez, Benjamin Alire Sáenz, and Luis Rodríguez. There were so many who helped me with my legal defense; you know who you are. There are people who were instrumental in those creative times when I was writing these stories: Suzanne Jamison; Deidre Sklar; the cast of my play *Elevators*; playwright Meghan Terry, who taught me that all plays are really musicals; Michael Jenkins and Bernie López from the New Mexico Arts Division; and my greatest angel, the indomitable and indefatigable Eleanor Broh-Kahn. There was also the anonymous donor who sent me $500 as a creative "grant," which helped me in a crucial time when I needed the support so badly. Your gift not only allowed me to pay the rent, it gave me hope that someday I would become an artist. Thanks to all who worked with me during that decisive and important time of my life, my sojourn in northern New Mexico.

My husband, Daniel Zolinsky, deserves accolades for his care, love, and constant and invaluable nurturing. He always knew what I needed, whether it was quiet, rest, a warm cat by my side, a good home-cooked meal, or onion rings in the middle of a hopeless night.

I am older now, the woman I remember my mother being when I was a teenager: robust, no-nonsense, a little too out-spoken, incorrigibly honest, apt to embarrass myself, others, a woman on fire with life. For this span of stories and for those people who believed in me during that cold winter I am grateful.

DENISE CHÁVEZ